JOLYNN KERR

Destiny's Window

Contents

Dedication

For my loving sister who I would be lost without.

About the Book

Surrounded by the lush, rich landscape of northern Minnesota, Dagmar Christianson, a young Norwegian girl, and her family fight to carve out a life in the ever changing times of the 1920s and through the Great Depression.

On the most perfect summer afternoon, young Dagmar's life is shattered as an epidemic of diphtheria ravages the Christian family claiming her beloved twin sister. Running from a mournful past, miserable present and uncertain future she finds herself lost in the arms of two brothers, each forever shaping her destiny. Always caught between the heartache of her past and the promise of her future, she searches for who she is and what she will do to protect her family.

Chapter 1

Summer 1923

Minaka Falls, Minnesota

"In the shadows of our grief and victories lies our destiny. We all have footprints in the past that follow us through the generations. Stomping, kicking, or marching us on to who we are or who we will become," Hans spoke his words softly as fifteen-year-old Dagmar listened to her father's words with pride and admiration.

"Olv was a good man, a good husband and father. He was a fine friend to everyone and a stranger to none. Let us give thanks for all that we have and that this horrible war will claim no more victims. Olv's lungs had been damaged by gas which had permeated the ground he had slept upon during the Great War far away, years before. His body was sent back to us dwindling and riddled with pain. Today we lay him to rest in this land we now call home," Hans said. The crowd stood hushed for a little while longer before each silently bid farewell to yet another true son of Norway.

"Hans, come join us down by the point. We give a toast to our Olv, one last time. We'll see you there. Ja?" His old friend Jorg tipped his cap, then ushered his family away.

"Ja, I will be along soon." Hans replied.

Dagmar stepped forward when the others had moved past. "Can I go with you, Papa?" Eager to spend some time with her father before he headed back to the family store, she pressed her body snugly to him hoping he would smile once again.

Papa held her close and kissed the top of her head. "No, my sweet one. You must go with the ladies and help Olv's family. There is much to be done and what I do is man's business," he said.

Dagmar sighed in disappointment but knew her fate was sealed. Sealed from the very day of her birth. Men were men and women were women, and it seemed to her to be a very unfair balance. "Please Papa, I'll stay out of the way and be so quiet you won't even know I'm there," she begged.

"It is for the best. Now go as I asked," Papa said, looking more stern.

A slight breeze blew from across the clear blue lake as the sun hung high over the horizon. Hans, now a man, stood shoulder to shoulder with his childhood friends, struggling to hold back tears as they gathered among the white birch trees. Those who had returned from the Great War seldom spoke of the nightmares and scars inflicted upon them, but today they had buried another one of their own. Now there were only seven.

"Skal, to Olv." Magnus raised his glass, and they each clinked twice in a salute to their old friend. Aquavit, a spirit made of a mix of grain and potatoes, once drunk by Viking warriors, was saved for special occasions. Theirs was a quiet, hardworking, pious culture, brought from the old country by their parents and grandparents before them. Mostly farmers and loggers, they were lured to America by the letters of those before them.

Land in the old country was scarce. Famine and hardship had forced many to make their way by steam liners, then by train through unfamiliar lands and customs. Homesteads or cheap plots sold by the railroads to help build the new towns were a dream they could not resist. Others came to pan for gold and fortune, or to cut the great timbers.

"Skal!" shouted Magnus once more. It was the Norwegian way.

The men settled in the lush green grass, perched against trees or a few scattered boulders near the shore's edge.

"Did you hear? They no longer want us to do our church service in Norwegian." Krause frowned as he looked about for signs of mutual scorn. Everyone began to mumble and grumble. "Nei, nei, no!" the shouts rang out.

"Olv's widow, Helena, is giving up the farm and heading to the city." Another round of forlorn comments settled in.

"All that glitters is not gold. The city is a haven of sinners and ruffians," Nils sighed. "We must do something. Our customs and ways are disappearing. Soon you won't be able to tell us from the Swedes or Finns," he said in exasperation.

Dagmar hid behind the big maple tree and listened as the men clinked their glasses and grumbled on. Her papa's head, hung low in sadness, brought tears to her eyes. She knew life had been hard for her father. Her grandfather and uncle had traveled far to come to his land, fleeing hard times in Norway. Papa had told her grandfather to cut the great soft pines that reached to the heavens to build the small cabin on the edge of lake, and later the bigger house as the family grew. He farmed the land where winters were hard, but it was their land and their hope that kept them going. She watched her papa stand once again and speak.

"We need to let go of the agonies and wounds of the past," Hans spoke in his usual voice of calm determination. "We have survived and endured much, but there is hope. I pray that humanity has learned a very harsh lesson and we will move forward in peace. There is such a great wonder in this country and much to offer our children. We, the ones who remain, are bound by our honor, courage, and tradition to not only survive, but to prosper. Today we must pledge to ourselves and one another, no matter where we are or what the need, We, The Seven, will stand strong together as one. We know not if victory or grief lie ahead, but if I need your help or you mine, we, The Seven, will be there. We are a family. It is the Norwegian way."

Dagmar slipped away carrying those words with her. "We are family," she whispered with pride aloud. "I'm a good Norwegian and one day I will protect my family, just like Papa and The Seven. It is the Norwegian way!" she shouted as her steps distanced her from the men and closer to home, her home where Mamma and the love and safety of her family waited. It was the Norwegian way.

Chapter 2

June 1923

Dagmar squealed with delight, as the miniature milk bottles scattered about in every direction. The Minaka Falls First Lutheran Church bazaar and picnic were in full swing, and it was a beautiful day for everyone to enjoy.

"Dagmar, you won. You won!" her twin sister, Myrtle, proclaimed. "That will show Lars who's the best thrower." They laughed in unison, as they always did. Lars was their older brother, but only by a year. The two sisters were inseparable. She and Myrtle did everything together, including annoying and challenging their beloved brother. Then there was Olga, the stunning beauty and demanding baby of the Christianson family. She was a handful on the best of days.

"Oh, my goodness, which prize should I choose?" Dagmar stepped back to take in the full view of her possibilities when she first felt him standing just behind her. She stood her ground with her feet planted firmly in the dirt. She was the stubborn twin. In a family of six, holding one's place was a full-time endeavor. Surely, he would do the gentlemanly thing and move away. He leaned in closer, and she caught the fresh fragrance of sandalwood soap. Dagmar bit her bottom lip and continued to ignore him.

"Take the bear over there," Harry whispered. His arm brushed up against her. She felt a strange tingle as the warmth of his breath engulfed her senses. He pointed to the one on the right. "He has the same dark, intriguing eyes as you."

The heat rose in her cheeks. Myrtle was the pretty twin. The one all the boys flocked around, vying for her attention. She was the smart twin with little use for such nonsense. She felt her knees wobble and held her breath tight. Dagmar nodded, and the bear was hers. Without turning to say a word, she knew he was gone in an instant.

Myrtle watched her sister in silence. The blush on her cheeks told her all she needed to know. She leaned in close, just as Harry had done. "He's a handsome one. Don't you think?" She paused and then added, "That's the new bank president's son. He has an older brother, George, who is just as handsome."

Dagmar scrambled to rein in the unfamiliar emotions. "Oh, Myrtle," she sighed. "I don't care if he is as handsome as a crowned prince or even a king or something, he's no gentleman."

Myrtle smiled the most radiant of smiles. "I think the banker's prince likes you."

Dagmar shifted her feet and raised her chin in defiance. "Hush," Dagmar demanded as she attempted to hide her obviously confused pleasure. "Let's go see what time the minister wants us to sing," putting an end to any further discussion of all prizes of the day, including the cuddly bear with the intriguing eyes or the handsome prince, she thought.

Helga Christianson sat under the red maple tree on the edge of the picnic grounds with her sister Hilda. "Hans will be concerned," she said to her sister. "He lost his dear parents to the influenza epidemic during the winter of 1919. So many died so quickly. It was frightening."

"I know dear." Hilda pressed the newspaper article flatly on the table. She hunched over to shade her eyes from the noonday sun and squinted to read the fine print. "It says here that there have been a large number of diphtheria cases in Duluth and the majority are children."

"Children? Dear Lord," Helga shook her head in disbelief.

Hilda continued to read further down the article, her voice even more serious now. "Patients may first have signs of a fever, also followed by respiratory struggles, coughing with a harsh almost barking sound. The neck and face may become swollen. Oh Lord, it's very contagious and all patients should be immediately quarantined." Hilda covered her hand over her mouth.

"We must ask Reverend Elgin to pray for everyone," Helga said. The look of fright was unmistakable on the sisters' faces.

"Mamma," Dagmar called as she and Myrtle approached the table.

Helga gave Hilda a look of warning not to frighten her children. If sickness and grief were to come, they would find out soon enough.

Hilda crinkled the newspaper clipping and tucked it safely away in her pocket.

"God morgen, Auntie Hilda." Myrtle said while hugging her aunt, then smiling to Mamma.

"Yes, good morning, my dear nieces," Hilda said, obviously pleased with Myrtle's gesture of respect. Her sister's girls were becoming such beautiful, well-mannered, and delightfully happy young women. The twins were each stunning in their own way. Myrtle had a slender face with massive flowing curls dancing in the gentle breeze. Her eyes were soft and had a kindness that radiated from her soul. Dagmar was taller and was the spitting image of her mother, with brownish blonde hair, sparkling, intriguing eyes and a smart wit about her. So many of the young no longer even attempted to speak their language.

"You should move these girls to town," Hilda tapped her sister's leg, while looking at the girls for approval. "There are so many more opportunities and options for them than there are on the farm. Young, handsome callers would tote flowers in hand for these lovely ones. Besides," she leaned in as if it were some great secret, "you and I could spend some more time together now that the children have grown, and Hans could tend his store better. I hear he is doing well."

"Ja," Mamma said, "he is a good hardworking man."

"We came to get you. Papa doesn't want you to miss us singing and we're going to sing something special for you." Myrtle and Dagmar chatted past what had become Auntie Hilda's favorite topic, now that her own children had both moved to the city. Helga and Hilda stood from their chairs, with the article tucked safely away. They strolled quietly across the grassy lawn towards the festivities of the day, leaving their concerns behind.

Lars, Harry, and George leaned over the hood of a new 1923 machine. "She's a beauty," Lars said.

"Yes, she is," Harry said.

George jabbed him in the side, grateful Lars didn't notice his brother's thoughts were focused on the young ladies crossing the open lawn. He wondered which beauty had caught his brother's eye. Both were lovely.

"Oh, I'm sorry," Harry said. He shifted his eyes back to where they belonged and after giving George a devilish grin. "How fast do you think she goes?"

George shook his head at his charming young brother and then said, "I'm not really sure, but…"

George's words were cut off by the sudden intrusion of his father's presence. "She's meant to travel thirty to thirty-five miles an hour. I've had her over sixty, but don't tell my wife." He laughed. Harry and George stood almost at attention at the sound of their father's voice. "You boys don't smudge the paint or there will be hell to pay." Karl Hanson had paid a good penny for the new motorcar. Over seven hundred dollars' worth of good pennies, which was twice the price of the new Model T and nearly half of most men's wages for the year. He cast them a stern look and headed for the shade tent reserved for the local Masonic lodge.

"Don't mind him," Harry said. "Must have woken up with a burr in his shoe again. He such an ass."

"Harry," George snapped. "You're the burr when you can't just ignore him. He likes to brag and make you angry.

You're like two bulls, always locking horns." George cut the unpleasant conversation off with an intense look.

Although five years younger and Harry's newly announced best friend, Lars was clearly more like George in temperament. Harry was young and had a certain charm. He was incredibly good looking, with the face and build of Apollo, but his impulsive urges and raging temper had yet to be reeled in and he was hoping Lars would provide some needed balance.

"Are you headed to university next year, Lars?" George asked.

"I wish I was," Lars replied. Papa will most likely want me to help run the store. Things are going really well these days. The farmers are producing more and more products. We can hardly handle what they have. And there are new gadgets becoming available every day. The ladies flock to the store to see the new catalogues or the newest fashions. These are exciting times, but university, that's my dream."

"Can't your sisters help in the store?" George asked.

"If all the pretty girls are going to be there, maybe I should come help," Harry said.

Lars chuckled. "My sisters are great, but like me, are in their last year of school. Myrtle already has them lining up at the door for Papa's permission to court her. She'll marry well," he said, beaming with pride. "Dagmar is the smart one. She has done well in school and will finish up this year top of our class, but I suppose there will be plans for her as well. That leaves me. University would be grand," he said with a look of disappointment, "but I have responsibilities."

In the distance, the sound of beautiful voices filled the air. Myrtle and Dagmar sang of love and joy for their family, happiness, and peace. They were the epitome of their times, young and hopeful. The 1920s were the decade of growth and plenty. Time stood still in that moment, wrapped in its optimistic innocence.

"Help! Help! He can't breathe!" Ingrid Anderson shouted from the center of the crowd. Her husband coughed and gasped for air. "Please, please. Where is the doctor?" she pleaded. He collapsed to the ground as the onlookers gawked in confusion.

Helga looked at Hilda in terror and shock, clutching and crumbling the article in her hand. "God help us," she mumbled aloud.

Chapter 3

Two weeks later

The last day of school had finally arrived, but twelve-year-old Olga was none too happy. "Wait for me. You guys are supposed to wait for me," Olga whined once again. "I'll tell Papa you left me behind."

Dagmar and Myrtle stopped in the middle of the dusty road. Their arms were clutched in their usual best friend, sisterly stance. They both stopped, turned, and looked back at Olga. It was a long walk to the farm from the schoolhouse, but one they had become accustomed to.

"Stop being such a baby, Olga!" Myrtle shouted. "We're tired of stopping for you. We want to go finish our chores and swim in the pond before supper." Myrtle's words were growing less and less patient with her little sister.

"I'm going to tell Papa you two talk about boys at the pond," Olga put her hands on her hips in satisfaction. "I saw Dagmar making googly eyes at Harry Hanson at recess too," she added, just to further her point.

"And I'll tell him you failed your spelling test," Myrtle calmly replied.

"I hate you, Myrtle Christianson. I wish you were dead," she snapped back in anger. "Just go on. I don't care. Both of you smell like cow poop, anyway. Does Harry like cow poop, Dagmar?" Olga giggled, feeling vindicated.

Myrtle and Dagmar looked at one another, nodded, and raced on to the gate of the farmhouse. Huffing and puffing from their little sprint. "That ought to teach the little cry baby snitch," Dagmar said.

Myrtle pushed back the gate. Mounted in the center for all to see, it read, Christianson, with 'We The Seven' boldly below their name. Myrtle paused for a moment, remembering Papa's stories of courage, loyalty, and family. "Let's just give her a minute," and they waited, knowing it was the right thing to do.

"Oh Myrtle, I wish I could be more like you," Dagmar said. "You're just like Papa, always doing the right thing and helping everyone. Olga tries my patience and riles me up like no one else." When they finally reached the house, Mamma greeted each with her usual kiss on the forehead and loving smile.

Mamma did her best not to show the panic that raced in her heart. "You have a fever, my little one," Mamma prayed it was just a simple summer cold.

Olga frowned with a little pout, "I haven't felt well all day and spelling was really hard," she said and nuzzled her head to her mother's chest.

After Olga was immediately put to bed, Dr. Jensen was called, and Mamma ushered everyone else out of the house. "I'm sure it's nothing, but let's take no chances. It may be contagious," she sighed.

Several hours passed with everyone but Olga and Mamma

having a picnic supper outside. At last, the doctor's dusty old Model T rattled up the path from the front gate. He climbed out grabbing his small black bag behind him and stuffed something in his back pocket.

Mamma watched from the window and gasped when she saw the green quarantine flag hanging from his pocket. Oh Lord, she thought, clutching her apron in her hands. The Berges, two farms down and several families closer to town had been stricken. Diphtheria. Mamma cringed at the thought. "Please God, no," she pleaded softly, rushing to the door.

"God dar, doctor." Mamma's fears deepened at the sight of her old friend's exhaustion.

"Helga," with a firm nod he greeted her back.

Mamma led him to the back bedroom where Olga had been placed, snuggled in the warmth and love of Mamma's coziest quilts.

"Let me see, young lady," the doctor began. It wasn't long before he directed Mamma out of the room. "I'm sorry, Helga. It's diphtheria." He paused a moment to allow his words to sink in but seeing her panic he rushed to calm her. He placed his hand with a gentle touch on her shoulder. "Her symptoms are mild, but you are going to have to watch her. She needs to stay still. Keep her warm and the rest of the family must stay away."

Mamma raised her hand to her mouth. "I must tell Hans, "she said with tears in her eyes.

"No Helga, I'll tell Hans. You've been exposed and will need to care for her. I'll check Hans and the other children. If they are okay, they'll need to stay down at the old cabin. Don't let her out of bed and I'll be back tomorrow. I'll leave instructions and a tonic on the kitchen table after I check the others for any symptoms. We're going to have to be careful. I'm sorry, Helga," he said patting his dear friend's shoulder once again.

The doctor left with at least the hopes that no one else was showing any signs of illness. Papa and the other children moved to the old cabin he and his parents had once stayed in before the big house was built. His parents had lived there as Mamma and Papa's family grew. In 1919, the influenza epidemic had taken both of them within a week's time. Now Papa used it as his fishing get-away, a place of peace and familiar memories.

Lars watched Papa with concern. "I think everything will be fine, Papa," he said, sitting at the small table where they now shared their meals. "Mamma will take good care of Olga and the girls, and I will help to do the chores and anything else you need," he said trying to reassure his father.

"It will be fine," Hans said. "Keep the girls busy. Not to worry." He was proud of his young son who was kind and obedient.

Dagmar rushed in the cabin door. "Papa, Mr. Peterson is down by the gate calling for you. He's brought a basket of goods and wants to talk to you."

Hans walked down towards the front gate where the green quarantine flag hung. "Jorge, stay back! Don't you see the flag? No one can come in, nor can we leave," he shouted from a safe distance.

"Ja, I know Hans, but we will help."

Hans remembered back to the day when they had made their pledge. The day of Olv's funeral. Tears welled in his eyes, thankful for all his blessings.

"I'm leaving a basket with some fresh breads, cheese, and jams. Arne wants to know if he can get your keys to the store.

His Katrina will take care of things until this is over." Jorge waited for Hans to respond.

"Jorge, that is too much," Papa's voice quivered as he spoke.

Jorge laughed, "Now Hans, don't act like those stubborn Swedes. This will be done with or without those keys. Tomorrow one of the other Seven will bring more. If you need anything, leave a note. We are here to help, as you would be for us. Remember, we are The Seven," he said before shouting again. "The key, Hans! Where is the key?"

Hans looked at his old friend. They had been through so much, childhood, war, and sickness. "Look above the door and I thank you, my friend!" Hans called out. "I thank you."

Just over a week had passed, and the doctor was prepared to pull the quarantine poster from the front door. "Olga is fine, Helga. She's a good strong girl."

Mamma breathed a sigh of relief. "Thank you, Dr. Jensen."

"Fredrik," he replied. "I gave you your first kiss as a young girl, Helga. If you hadn't fallen for that handsome rascal, Hans, I'd have courted and married you myself."

Mamma blushed like a naïve schoolgirl and said, "You're right, Fredrik. You're a fine man and Ida is a lucky woman to have you. I thank you with all my heart for seeing us through this. Olga is so very precious to us."

He smiled. "Rest now Helga. The rest of the family can come home." The words barely left his mouth, and they heard a knock. There was a slow creaking sound of the door opening and Myrtle's body trembled as she staggered in.

16

"Mamma, I don't feel well." She swayed and reached for her mother, before collapsing on the floor. Mamma and the doctor rushed to her side.

"Myrtle!" Mamma screamed, falling to her knees.

The doctor raised her up. Myrtle struggled to speak, "My throat hurts." She coughed and the sickening odor of sweetness and diphtheria and fear filled the air.

Chapter 4

J une 1923

Dagmar tapped on the windowpane to the small corner bedroom. "Myrtle, Myrtle. Are you sleeping?" She had waited days before Mamma and the doctor would allow her to see her sister. It was the longest she had ever been parted from her sister, who now appeared to be resting peacefully. Dagmar was relieved.

Less than a week before when Myrtle had collapsed on that afternoon, everyone was in shock. They had been working in the vegetable garden that morning as Mamma had taught them, turning the soil, pulling the weeds, and gently watering one by one what would be the bounty of a summer long harvest, then autumn before the snow covered the cold frozen Minnesota ground. Later, they chatted and giggled while stitching on pillow covers Mamma had specially made for them. Each embroidered tiny flowers and whimsical hearts, all of which would be neatly pressed, folded, and placed safely away in their wedding chests to grace the homes they would one day make with their own families.

Dagmar closed her eyes and remembered, "All my flowers are lavender," Myrtle said. "Papa ordered these special threads especially for me in every variety of purple available. Violets, pansies, and lilacs, they'll be so beautiful." There was a beauty and gentleness about her sister that Dagmar admired. No one was as kind and lovely as Myrtle.

A tap on the window broke the trance Dagmar had been under. Mamma waved her hand and blew a small kiss from her lips. Myrtle was awake and looking somewhat pale but stronger, Dagmar thought, or maybe it was a wishful prayer, but she was delighted her sister seemed to be recovering after so many days.

"I brought you lilacs. They're your favorite. I cut them from the big bush by the front porch." Dagmar paused, noticing the tears in her sister's eyes. Her face was swollen and still pale. Mamma had wrapped warm towels around her neck. Olga told her it helped ease the pain. Dagmar smiled, trying to hide her despair for her sister. "The doctor told Papa you're getting better. Please rest and I'll bring more flowers tomorrow." Myrtle raised her fingers scarcely above the quilt to wave goodbye and her eyes shut once more.

Days and days had passed, but Myrtle was finally looking more like herself. The swelling had gone down, and coughing was less often. Mamma was looking less worn. Auntie Hilda had come three days before. Mamma was furious. "You can't be here," she said. "It's very contagious."

Auntie Hilda tossed her satchel to the floor and spoke with determination. "Ja, and you are my only sister. My children are grown, and my dear husband has passed. It is you who needs me and I you." The decision was final. Auntie Hilda would stay.

Lars stood next to Dagmar and gave a brisk tap on the window. Mamma, Auntie Hilda, and Myrtle peered through the window looking far more rested than they had in days. Olga fidgeted around picking clover leaves in the grass but stood and bid them hello.

"I've brought you more lilacs!" Dagmar shouted out. Her sister waved and made a gesture of thanks with her hand to her heart and then to her lips. Dagmar and Lars smiled. Olga continued to search for the elusive lucky clover cluster.

"The lake has warmed up and everyone can't wait to see you at the Fourth of July picnic." Dagmar said. "If you are up to it, we are to sing at the opening ceremony."

"But only if you are well," Lars added. "I'm to read a poem for the Young Sons of Norway." They all laughed at such a thought. Lars didn't care for public speaking and singing was best left to his beautiful sisters.

Mamma adjusted and primped Myrtle's pillow trying to help her sit up. Myrtle strained to push herself forward, as she began what had become the all-too-familiar coughing. Auntie Hilda scurried to the side table, pouring a glass of water from one of Mamma's best pitchers. Everyone waited, but the coughing gripped Myrtle more and more violently with each gasping of breath.

Dagmar lunged forward to the glass. Her hands were pressed to the pane in desperation. "Myrtle. Mamma. Mamma help her. Stop it, Mamma. Stop it," she pleaded. Tears rolled endlessly down Dagmar's face, as Lars tried to pull her back.

"No! I need to help Myrtle!" Dagmar shouted, lashing, and pushing her brother way. "Myrtle! she screamed, "I love you. I love you. Please Myrtle. I love you," she sobbed.

"Go get Papa," Lars commanded to Olga who was still sitting in the grass in a stunned, motionless stupor. "Hurry. Go."

Suddenly, Myrtle clutched her hand to her chest, then fell back to her pillow. Mamma screamed. "No! No! Not my angel," before dropping to her knees taking Myrtle's hand and pressing her lips to it. "Please my darling, please don't leave us," she begged. Papa rushed into the room startled and helpless, wrapping his arms around his dear wife. Auntie Hilda turned and slowly, placing the glass of water back on the side table and then closed the lace curtains, as Dagmar's world swirled into darkness. Not even Papa could fix this.

Myrtle was buried two days later in the church cemetery. The headstone would come later and was to match Papa's parents' headstone. They were Dagmar's beastamor and morfar, but she could scarcely recall their faces. She had been so young, but now understood Papa's sadness, which would shroud all of them. The shadow of their grief would be a heavy, dark burden. The wives and families of The Seven rallied together, bringing food and comfort to the farm. Auntie Hilda did her best to greet fellow church goers, Masons, town, and farm folk alike, who came to give their condolences, each secretly praying their family would not be next.

Dagmar sat by the window watching the procession of despair arrive, one after the other. She touched the glass, feeling the coolness upon her fingers. Jerking them back as a sear of the pain singed her heart with the memory of that same coolness when she pleaded for… No, she just couldn't think anymore. She had barely spoken and refused to cry.

When Lars had lifted her from the ground beneath the bedroom window, he placed Myrtle's lilacs back in her arms and spoke in a whisper. "Come, Dagmar. Let's go inside. Mamma needs you now. Mamma needs you." Destiny's window was cruel that day and Dagmar was certain she would never love another as she had loved her sister.

Chapter 5

The Threads of the Christianson family unraveled ever so slowly, minute by minute. Days, nights, and months blended together into a cocoon of darkness, to be breached by no one. Papa busied himself tending the store, away from home and the painful reminders of all he had lost. Mamma grew thinner, paler, and older with each passing day. Lars and Olga stayed at school and with friends, each thankful for any distraction that came their way, but Dagmar seemed the one most adrift. She no longer sang at celebrations or in church. She finished her schoolwork and chores in silence, wrapped in a robe of despair.

"Dagmar." Harry leaned against the old maple tree just outside the schoolhouse. He waited to see if she would respond, look his way, or even slow down. Anything he could take as a sign. "Dagmar," he said louder and stepped forward reaching for her arm.

She was startled but seemed to have little concern for his presence. "Oh hello, Harry. I'm sorry, I didn't realize you were there." Dagmar looked down, straightened her books, and prepared to move on.

"Wait," Harry said, not realizing he had yet to release her arm. "I wanted to ask you something." He felt foolish and somehow ashamed that he had invaded her intense seclusion, but he had been waiting for her. Waiting months and months, almost since that first day at the church bazaar, he had been smitten with her. She stood her ground that day, refusing to budge an inch, unfazed and unimpressed by his presence. All the other girls swooned at his very existence, the handsome son of the rich banker, but Dagmar refused to even acknowledge him. Later, when she sang like a nightingale, he was the one to swoon. His heart stung as he watched her stare out the window of her father's automobile, lost in the shock and nightmare of her beloved Myrtle's death. He thought of his family. Never had there been that kind of loyalty and unquestionable love. Harry envied her and that love, but was certain she remained lost, even now. Shifting his stance, he could wait no more. "I wanted to know if you might consider going to the graduation dance with me?"

"No," Dagmar said.

Harry stood motionless watching her walking away from him, away from the world once again.

"Kicked you like a mule, little brother," George chuckled from behind.

"What do you know about mules?" Harry snapped, not bothering to turn and look at his older brother.

"I know that's a stubborn one and will not be any more than her daddy's store clerk."

Harry spun around and shoved his older brother. "Shut up, George. You sound like father now." Harry wasn't satisfied.

His brother was sprawled on the ground and looked like he had been punched in the face. He continued on, "You know nothing about her. Dagmar is smart, beautiful, kind, and loyal. She's fragile right now, but don't underestimate her. She's going to be an amazing woman one day."

"Okay, okay," George said getting up and dusting himself off. "I stand corrected, and I'll keep that in mind next time I see her, but the thing you better keep in mind is, father will never approve. I may know nothing about Dagmar or mules, but I know father."

Supper was late that night, as it so often seems to be these days. Papa sat at the head of the table with Mamma at the other end. Dagmar, Lars, and Olga sat in their usual chairs and Myrtle's chair had been placed against the wall. Papa was looking unusually cheerful. "I have big news," he said before grace was even said. "Mamma and I have been talking and we're going to rent out the farm and move to town."

Olga was the first to speak. "How wonderful," she said. "I'm sick of being stuck way out here. All of my friends live in town and there's just so much more to do. I could stay for choir and the drama teacher asked me to try out for a very important part," she batted her eyes and flipped her long curly hair back off her shoulder. "Not to mention that cold winter walk home. I missed almost an entire month of school this year, when the snow piled up nearly to the roofs."

Lars snickered. "Always the drama, Olga. It wasn't that bad, but it might be a pleasant change for Mamma. She'll be closer to Auntie Hilda." Lars and Papa had talked about Mamma's declining health. "Maybe change will be good for all of us," he said.

"How about you, Dagmar?" Papa said in an almost pleading voice. "Are you happy?"

There was a knock on the door, everyone turned to see who would come to call this late. Lars got up from the table and greeted their guest at the door.

Dagmar bit her lower lip and held her tongue for the moment, relieved to have been spared from the task of shouting at the top of her lungs all the reasons why moving to town was insane. This was their home.

"Sorry for being so late. Thought you folks would be done with supper by now," Roland Krog said.

"Goodness, goodness," Mamma said. "It's no trouble. Come sit. Would you like some stew?"

"No thank you, I've already eaten." He grabbed Myrtle's chair and dragged it to the table next to Lars.

Dagmar couldn't decide at that moment whether sitting in Myrtle's chair or the disgusting wink he gave Olga annoyed her most. Roland was at least ten years older than Olga and had no excuse to behave as such in front of Olga and her family. He was known to be a gambler, drinker, and womanizer. He was nothing like his papa or grandfather before him. She clenched her fists. Roland was a rogue, and this had to be stopped.

"My father and I heard rumors you may be renting your farm out."

Now Dagmar was certain there was no one she could possibly dislike more than Roland. "It hasn't been decided!" she exclaimed.

Papa coughed, clearing his throat as a gentle warning to his eldest daughter. "There is a possibility that may be true. I will speak with your papa tomorrow." That was a warning to both Dagmar and Roland that the discussion was over. Dessert was offered, but Roland was promptly on his way and the dishes were cleared.

Lars pulled Dagmar aside onto the front porch. "You need to stop being so selfish and burying your head in the past. Mamma isn't well here, and it's a lot for Papa to keep running in and out of town. He tends the store and does many of the tasks Mamma used to do. She is tired and sad. Auntie Hilda will help if we're in town."

"Mamma is fine," Dagmar insisted. Lars' tongue lashing had startled her. It was unlike him to raise his voice or offer criticism. She didn't like it one bit.

Lars crossed his arms and gave a bitter and sarcastic laugh. "She's not well and neither are you," he scorned. "You used to laugh and sing. You were the witty one, always getting us into fixes and then Myrtle would…" he let his words trail off.

Dagmar stormed away, retreating into her room. No one followed her, and she was thankful. She tossed and turned all night. She wasn't selfish, and she was just fine. Okay, Mamma hadn't been herself since Myrtle died, but how could she be, or anyone else for that matter? Now they wanted her to leave her home.

"What will be next?" she mumbled aloud. Why couldn't people just leave her alone? Why in the world would Harry Hanson ask her to a dance? She needed to think. She needed to talk to Myrtle. Everything was changing and changing way too fast. She shut off her light and pushed away the world, retreating into the darkness all alone.

Chapter 6

June 1924
"I'll be late. But tell Papa not to worry, I'll be fine!" Dagmar yelled back to Lars. She needed some space to be alone where no one told her what to think or who to be, and she knew the perfect place.

Dagmar sat down on the damp grass pressing her hand to the cool headstone. "Oh Myrtle, I miss you so much. I've brought you lilacs from your favorite bush near the front porch." She began her protest that had been brewing in her head and was aching to get out. "I'm going to complain to you, because no one else listens to me."

She loved being all alone in the cemetery. She felt free to tell Myrtle everything, just as she had always done, until… Until exactly one year ago today. Life had become one big blur at that time. She pushed herself through every day, wishing she could be left alone in solitude. Dagmar took another deep breath to clear her mind.

"Well, I finished school now, Myrtle. I was first in class for mathematics and second in reading, but now I'm lost. Papa is making us give up the farm and move into town. He said it will be easier for everyone and Mamma needs Auntie Hilda," she continued. "Mamma misses you so." Dagmar cut her thoughts short. She would not cry today, no matter what. She promised herself never to cry again on the night Lars had made her so angry, calling her selfish. She looked around to be certain she was still alone.

"If anyone is selfish, it's Lars. All he cares about is his friends and trying to get a scholarship to university. Olga is such a brat. She actually tried to get me to sing with her. Can you imagine? It doesn't matter, I'm never singing again. Ever. Why does everything have to change so much? One thing I'm hoping is Papa will change his mind about the farm. I don't want to move, not now, not ever." Dagmar felt the tears coming on and jumped to her feet. It was time to go home before she broke her promise not to cry. Nope, she was never going to cry again, never, ever. She knew she was being stubborn, but she just wasn't ready to move on. Not today, of all days.

Dagmar stopped at the front gate to the farm. "Christianson, We The Seven," she read aloud with great satisfaction. Her family name and their unity with the past always gave her the profound comfort of something greater than herself. She was part of a family, not just someone all alone lost in a sea of strangers. But lately she was feeling more and more alone. She walked towards the house admiring the pansies she and Mamma had recently planted. The familiar creak of the porch step made her smile. This was home, she thought, before noticing the note on the door. COME TO THE NEW HOUSE.

Opening the door, Dagmar let it spring wide. The house was empty. No tables, no chairs, nothing, nothing at all to say they had ever lived there. The emptiness overwhelmed her, but her anger made it certain she would once again keep her promise. Dagmar would not cry. "I won't cry, not today, not ever," she muttered kicking the dirt beneath her feet before she headed down the long, lonely road to town. She fumed in her anger.

Lars met her halfway on the road to town. He honked the horn and was amused when she jumped in surprise. "Hi, Sis!" he called out to her as he slowed, then stopped the car. Immediately he saw the look of darkness and anger. It was too late to take cover from the storm she was about to unleash, so he opened the car door.

Dagmar got into the vehicle, slamming the door behind her. The rage was apparent on her face, and she launched her attack on Lars. "Where are my things? Why is our home empty, and don't any of you know what day this is?" She pounded her fist on the dashboard.

"Settle down, Dagmar. Settle down. Let me explain…."

"There's no explaining!" she shouted and punched the dashboard once again. "I want my things. No one had a right to touch my belongings."

"I'm sorry, Dagmar. Papa found a couple of helpers who could only help today and honestly, he thought it would be better for Mamma to not stay one more night there. Especially tonight. She's not well," Lars said.

"What do you mean, she's not well?" Dagmar had seen Mamma getting thinner, paler, and weaker, but, oh God, maybe she was selfish. "What's wrong with her?"

Lars stared straight ahead at the road. "There is a new field of medicine called psychology. It studies how the mind works. When things happen to us, we each react differently. Mamma's mind and body have had a lot of struggles. She also has something known as rheumatoid arthritis." Lars paused to allow Dagmar time to take his words in. "Mamma's muscles and bones are very weak. When she was younger, her family was poor and malnourished. Myrtle's passing was the final trauma her mind and body could take. She is not well."

Dagmar couldn't believe what she was hearing. It wasn't possible things were that bad. How could she not have known? "Why didn't Papa tell us?" she asked.

Lars held tight to the steering wheel with one hand and ran his fingers through his hair with the other. "It's complicated," he said, still looking straight ahead. "There are new treatments every day, but they're expensive."

"What do you mean, expensive? I help Papa with the books. The store has done really well this year," Dagmar questioned.

"Like I said, it's complicated. When Myrtle was so sick, they were working on vaccines and treatments. We don't live in the city and we're not rich. These things take time. Just like Myrtle, Mamma's damage may have gone too far. She'll be…" his chest heaved as the words stumbled out. "She may be in a wheelchair very soon. She's just not well."

"Is there nothing we can do?" Dagmar pleaded.

"Papa is going to take her to the hot springs down in Georgia this summer. They'll be gone for several weeks, and we'll have to run things at the store. They're counting on us, and I'm counting on you."

The car rattled along on the road for what had already seemed like an eternity. "I'll help, Lars." Dagmar's voice was just above a whisper. She brushed a strand of hair from her face and sat up straight in her seat. "I guess it's better than looking for a husband, now that I'm finished with school."

Lars laughed, "Don't hold your breath. It won't be long

before Olga is shopping for both of you." They both laughed in unison until Lars' face turned serious. He turned for just a moment to face her. "I have a secret," he said.

Dagmar waited, praying it wasn't more bad news. "Tell me. Please, I want to know."

"I want to be a doctor."

Dagmar stared at her older brother. He was handsome, as young men go. He looked more like a younger version of Papa, tall with blondish wavy hair. Just like Papa, he was smart and a hard worker. Myrtle had taught him kindness and patience, but he could be stubborn like her. She took a deep breath and decided she couldn't quite recall when exactly he had stopped being her brother, the child, and became a man. "I'll help you, Lars. I'll help you," she said.

"If I don't get a scholarship, no one can help me." He sighed. "Plus, Papa is counting on me to help in the store."

"We'll figure it out, Lars. We're just like The Seven, we stick together. I'll handle Papa, you figure out how to get that scholarship." Dagmar brushed her fingers over the sign she had ripped from the gate of the farm. She turned and gazed out the window. Once again, she seemed to be watching the world moving past her, faster and faster, out of her control. "Drop me here by the lake. I need some time before I'm ready to call that place home. I just need some time."

Chapter 7

Dagmar walked along the rocky shoreline of the lake which extended on for miles. There was an insatiable demand for more and more building timber, especially the tall, soft white pines that had grown for hundreds of years. They were huge, cut easily and floated effortlessly down the rivers to the sawmills. The once adjacent stands of massive timbers were gradually thinning and forever changing the magnificent landscape. Papa had complained that this was not a good thing, and eventually there would be a price to pay for such greediness. Dagmar sighed as she settled in, dangling her feet over the small cliff that jetted out over the water's edge, taking in the freshness of earth and pungent smell of the pines.

The forest behind her and the blue, dazzling sky spread above the shimmering lake brought her strength. She tossed the pebbles and various stones, one by one, that she had collected along the way. There was a price to pay for everything, she thought, and longed for the simpler days of her childhood.

"Are you trying to win another bear or are you picking a fight with the trout?" Harry teased from behind her.

Dagmar held herself steady, trying not to show her annoyance. She had come to her special place to seek peace and solitude where no one could bother her. Things had to be figured out, what the future was going to be, how she was going to help Lars, what would happen to Mamma, what she was going to do herself. She needed quiet. She had to figure these things out. What would be right in her heart and mind? Now here was Harry, another distraction. Another problem.

"What are you doing here, Harry? This is my place. Nobody's supposed to be here."

Harry chuckled, "Sorry, I didn't know you owned the lake."

"You're so funny," Dagmar said. "You know exactly what I mean. I've got a lot on my mind and I'm just trying to figure some things out. Not all of us have your tranquil, extravagant life."

Harry sat down next to her. "Here, this will help," he said and handed her a flask of whiskey.

"No, thank you," she said, turning away.

"Suit yourself, if you're too scared."

Dagmar grabbed the flask from his hand, "I'm not afraid of anything," she snipped at him, knowing full well it was a boldfaced lie. She was afraid of everything, her mournful past, miserable present, and uncertain future. But the one thing she wasn't afraid of was Harry Hanson.

"Whoa, slow down. That's a man's drink." Harry attempted to retrieve his flask before she emptied its contents.

Dagmar coughed, choking slightly as she sputtered her words out. "Of course, it's a man's drink. Everything belongs to men," she said in anger. "We women just marry you, clean your houses, have your children, and watch them die. And then we die. You men run everything, go to university, and tell us where to live." She tried to jump to her feet, in an attempt to put as much distance as possible between them and her ever-mounting humiliation.

Harry immediately grabbed her and kissed her firmly on the mouth. He smiled as he saw the fiery of the old Dagmar come alive. "I'm sorry. It was the only way I knew to shut you up," he said, still grinning.

"Let me go, you idiot," she fumed and pushed away from him. Struggling to straighten her dress and dignity, she began her attack, "You're just a spoiled, rich, handsome boy, but that doesn't give you the right…"

Harry's face turned to one of anger and Dagmar froze, suddenly fearful.

"You think you know everything, Dagmar, but you don't know me!" Harry shouted. "All anyone ever sees is our big house and fine car. I thought you were different. My father is an important man at the bank and is considered a pillar of the community, but that's not all he is." Harry paused, seething in anger. "He drinks. That was his whiskey. I stole it. I'm going to kill him one day. Do you hear me? I'm going to kill him!"

Dagmar jumped to her feet, filled with panic and fear. He was right; she didn't know him and needed to get out of there, now. She stepped back away but felt the ground give way beneath her.

Harry had in one swift motion leaped to his feet, reaching to grab Dagmar. She clutched his hand, as if her life depended on it. "I can't swim, Harry! Please, help me. Help me. Don't let me fall."

"It's okay, Dagmar. I've got you. I promise I won't let go

of you." Harry pulled her dangling body with all his strength. "You're safe now. "You're safe," he said with his arms securely around her as they fell back to the ground.

"You frightened me," she said, trying to sit up.

"You're shivering. I'm so sorry," he whispered and reached for the blanket he had brought to sit on. He wrapped it over her shoulders and pulled it snuggly in front of her. He struggled for his eyes to meet hers. "My father hurts my mother, brother, and me." His voice trembled. "I'm so sorry. I never meant to harm you. I'll never, ever hurt you again. I promise. Do you want me to take you home now?" Harry looked away in shame.

"No," Dagmar said, as she turned his face back to her. "I'm fine," she whispered as her thumb brushed across his stubbled chin then tracing his lips. Nestling against his chest, she felt a wave of warmth as her fingers innocently slipped beneath his shirt feeling the beat of his heart. "Harry don't ever leave me. Everyone I love, leaves…."

Harry's kisses silenced her sorrow. "I'll never leave you." His body pressed against hers, as he laid her to the grass, kissing her slender neck, seeking, and longing for comfort and peace.

Dagmar yielded to him. Not questioning, for the first time she forgot about Myrtle, Mamma, Papa, Lars, and Olga. She didn't care where she would live, or what her life would bring. She knew at that moment she would love Harry and only him for all of her life.

They melted into an intimacy that she knew could damn them one day, but tonight under the cover of darkness surrounded by the canopy of the remaining forest, they would cast their pain away. They would neither rush nor fumble their way but bask in the beauty and innocence they had been blessed with and pledged to never doubt or betray it.

Dagmar rushed into the new house prepared for Papa's displeasure. He sat by the fire. The light was low, and everyone had long since gone to their beds for the night, but Papa waited. He looked calm when he asked her to come sit with him near the fire.

"Sit, my sweet one," he said. "I know this is a difficult day for you, but please do not stay out in the darkness like that again. You are a beautiful young woman now and your family worried so. You must learn to think of others now." He spoke in a firm tone. "You are not a child anymore." His voice softened. "I know change does not come easy for you. I want you to be happy and you must look to the future," he said.

Dagmar sat quietly, listening to Papa's advice, then stood up above him, now a grown woman. She kissed him on the top of the head. "I know, Papa. Do not worry about me any further. I have sorted out my worries and I am fine once again. She hugged her papa as she had done as a young child so many times before and then walked to her new bedroom wondering if Harry thought her beautiful as well.

Chapter 8

Banners of red, white, and blue flapped in the occasional breeze as the band played the now familiar, American March King, Sousa's, tunes over and over throughout the day. The grand Fourth of July picnic gathered the inhabitants of the surrounding area, near and far. The country was prospering and so was the small town of Minaka Falls. New businesses were on a steady rise as the population continued to grow. It was a glorious day to enjoy the celebration and the simple pleasures of the day.

Dagmar and Harry spread their blanket and luncheon cloth across the grass under a silver maple tree, further from the noise and crowd.

"It's such a beautiful day," she said, arranging the containers of food she had primped and fussed over all morning.

Harry leaned back against the tree trunk and marveled at her beauty. She had somehow softened his anger and given him peace and a new sense of direction. Things had quieted down at home. He was working at the bank for the summer. His older brother George had secured a position in Duluth. His father was pleased his mother had been elected to be the new ladies auxiliary church secretary. The business of the bank was going well, and new accounts were opening every day.

Harry and Dagmar slipped away to their secret heaven down by the lake but were careful not to stir any gossip. He dreaded the thought of going away to university so soon but was certain his happiness depended on it. Once he was done, he could do as he pleased. His grandmother was wise enough not to trust his father and had seen to a trust for his education, which left him free of his father's clutches. George was already moving away to Duluth. Harry would play nicely until the summer was over, and he would be out of his father's reach.

"Where are you, my charming prince?" Dagmar chuckled seeking to break his far-away trance.

"Don't forget handsome. You said I was handsome," he teased before securing his long-awaited kiss.

"Don't forget spoiled," she said before tapping his roving hands. "I've made you some special treats, krumkake and butter cookies, but first, some of Mamma's pickled herring, fresh bread, and cheese. I filled the krumkake cookies with lots of whipped cream for you."

He rubbed his belly in exaggeration. "I just might sink our boat in the race today, if I eat all that." And they laughed in the moment's merriment.

"Papa said I could share lunch with you, but I must spend the afternoon with family. Lars can escort me to the fireworks. "I'm hoping I'll see you there," Dagmar said, handing him a cool lemonade.

She had scarcely spent much time alone with Harry since the night they had laid in each other's arms. Dagmar worked in the store, balancing accounts, and stocking goods. Mamma's trip to the hot springs had left her feeling somewhat better and stronger. Harry's father kept him busy with one task after another.

"You know I leave in a few weeks," he said.

"I know," she replied, "but we can write to one another. Maybe you'll be home for Christmas break." Dagmar's eyes sparkled with excitement.

"Of course, I'll write but remember, I'm taking a heavy load right from the start. If I work hard, I can finish a year early." Harry could wait no longer and pulled her tightly to him, cascading kisses down her slender neck, feeling the heat rise within him.

Abruptly he stopped, seeing his father staring at them across the field. His body tensed and he defiantly kissed her. It was long and passionate, just to be certain his father understood. He was a man and would make his own choices. Soon he would be free from his father's reach and the old man might as well get used to it.

The day drifted on, filled with music, dancing, and food. Neighbor after neighbor were elated to see Dagmar and the entire Christianson family smiling and once again enjoying the day. Olga sang, danced, and flirted her way through the festivities. Lars and Papa enjoyed the afternoon with the boat races and lumbering contests. Mamma, Auntie Hilda, and Dagmar caught up on the latest gossip in town, who was courting who and was engaged. Who was a good match was quite another story.

Seeing a little color back in Mamma's cheeks was nice, but Dagmar was becoming more and more aware that Lars' diagnosis of Mamma's condition was correct. Papa had hired a young girl to help Mamma so Dagmar could help at the store and Olga could go to school and attend her music lessons.

The band was slowing its tunes, and the sun left a tinge of orange and red settling above the horizon.

"Lars will stay with you girls for the fireworks. Mamma grows tired and needs to go home. Please don't be too late, my dears," Papa said as he hugged each of them closely.

Dagmar looked around waiting for Harry to return. Lars and Olga wandered off in various directions, leaving her alone with her thoughts. She closed her eyes and felt the gentle breeze rustling through the trees.

So much had happened in the last month, she welcomed the moment to examine her thoughts. The new house had not been so bad, and she enjoyed the business of the town. Mamma seemed happier near her sister and Papa announced he may sell the store, if he could get the financing for a new venture. Lars had yet to hear news of his scholarship but was settling in with his disappointment. Harry's mentioning his leaving saddened her, but she had decided to face her situation head on. Three years was a long time to wait for him to graduate, let alone establish him, but nothing would dissuade her.

Papa had trusted her with the accounts at the store, perhaps he would in his new venture as well. She could help Papa and surely, he would pay her a little more now that she was a grown woman, no longer nearly a schoolgirl. She would nest away the extra money for the life she dreamed of.

Women were beginning to work in all sorts of jobs. Although

women teachers were forced to leave their positions, once they were married and most women were maids and housekeepers. Still, women now had the right to vote, and the Great War had seen thousands of women trained to be nurses and thousands more worked in factories when needed. More secretaries, switchboard operators, and salesclerks were needed in a growing economy. Dagmar saw her possibilities as endless.

The first crackle of the sparkling fireworks illuminated the sky and smoke drifted high above as the grand finale had long silenced and still, no Harry. The heat of the day was lingering, but she shivered and felt anxiety, the puffs of smoke were fading away, one by one, and so were all her dreams. Where was Harry?

Chapter 9

Mamma and Papa sat at the morning breakfast table. The enticing aroma of cinnamon and almond filled the air. They gently stirred their porcelain cups filled with good strong coffee and just a dab of milk, it was the Norwegian way.

"I think it's a good option, Helga," Papa said. "Arne Krog has his share of the money. If we sell the store and I go to the bank, we will have our share. The country is growing so quickly now. Everyone wants to buy a new car, not just rich people. It's time to look to the future."

"What's this?" Lars said, as he and Dagmar settled into their chairs. "You're really going to sell the store?"

"It's up to Papa," Mamma said.

Papa could hardly contain his excitement. He shifted in his chair. "Sit, Lars. It's so exciting. I'll tell you everything. Gustermen has been pestering me for years to buy the store. Yesterday at the picnic he made me a fine offer. Arne has been looking for a partner to open a new car dealership, right in the center of town. It's the best location and right now people must go all the way to the city to buy a car or truck. Think of all the lumber trucks and family cars we could sell. It's a sure thing. And Lars, if you don't get that scholarship you are hoping for, you can be my right-hand man. We'll make a fortune. Arne is sure of it."

"Papa, you know I have plans, but if they don't work out, I'm sure I could help. But just until I get my scholarship. I'm going to university, one way or another," he said.

"Ja, ja. I know, son, but this has a real future."

Dagmar sighed to herself. Future, she thought. Her future never showed up to the fireworks last night. She had tossed and turned all night and really had no patience for this business talk. "Lars, did you see Harry last night after you brought me home?"

"No," Lars said. "I thought he was meeting you for the fireworks. That's why you were so grumpy. I'm sure it's his father. He probably put a stop to that. He keeps a tight hand on everything Harry and George do."

Dagmar had listened to some of the frightful tales Harry had struggled with. His father drank in secrecy and was often violent and abusive. There was the public Karl and then there was the monster behind closed doors, to be feared and catered to. Lars was right, this couldn't be Harry's fault. He had promised to meet her and oh so much more.

"We may see him at the bank," Papa said. "Lars and I will go see Mr. Hanson before lunch. Arne and Guestermen are waiting for my answer." He pushed his chair back and rose, signaling all was decided.

"Lars, let me write a quick note for you to give Harry. I won't be long. I promise," Dagmar rushed away her thoughts swirling about. My dearest Harry, she began constructing the letter in her head. She just had to see him.

Karl Hanson nodded to his secretary to show his next clients into his office. He was the epitome of public decorum and had mastered keeping a cool head in all things concerning business, but the Christiansons were pushing his boundaries. Seething in anger, since yesterday's catastrophic fight with his son, Harry, Karl gritted his teeth.

"Hans, Lars, what can I do for you?" he said, motioned them to have a seat.

Hans explained to him the purpose of their visit, covering every detail in the most positive manner. "Arne has his share and with the sale of the store, I will only need so much."

"Hmm," Karl said, sitting behind his enormous desk, meant to impress and intimate those who dared to enter his kingdom. "Perhaps we can help. The bank allows me a great deal of discretion in these matters."

Hans and Lars straightened in the hard wooden chairs looking hopeful.

"But..." Karl let the word dangle in the air. "I'll need some assurances."

"Ja, ja, yes," Hans said. "I'm good for my word, just ask anyone."

"I'm afraid I'll need more than that," Karl said, enjoying his ability to manipulate his power to best benefit himself. If he played this right, he'd be rid of the Christiansons and their little store clerk daughter. He'd have Harry right where he wanted him.

"I'll need to hold the deeds to your house and the farm, for that kind of money. But as you said, you're good for your word, so you'll have them back in no time. These are wonderful times. A car dealership is an excellent idea. It's just a minor detail," he added.

"And Lars, I'm on the board at the university. When we finish up this business, I'll call and see what I can do about that scholarship." The sudden pleading look on Lars' face told him his trap was set. It was a good day to be the only banker for miles around and a good day to put Harry in his place. He gloated to himself. "I'll get the papers and we can make this a deal right now," Karl waited for the trap to snap.

"I'll bring you the deeds straight away," Hans said, offering a good firm handshake.

Lars and Papa arrived at home just before the noon meal with cash in hand. "I've no time to eat now," Papa said. "I must go see Guestermen and give Arne the money to put down on the property lease. We'll have to do some renovation and purchase our stock. Take care of the deeds for me, Lars," Papa said. He kissed Mamma goodbye and hurried off.

"Did you see Harry? Did you give him my note?" Dagmar had waited patiently enough for Papa to leave. "Lars?"

Lars reached into his pocket, knowing full well he hadn't even given it a thought. "Harry wasn't there, and I thought it best to deliver it to his home. His father is all business at the bank," he said trying to not appear as if he were lying. His sister always knew when he was lying.

"Okay," Dagmar sighed, as Lars closed the door and began his brisk march down the street.

Walking to the window, Dagmar watched Lars heading back

to the center of town. She had an uneasy feeling noticing the dark clouds hovering in the distance. Summer storms were known to be dangerous. Last year a tornado touched down not two miles away and demolished an entire farm along with their entire crop of sweet corn. This didn't feel like a tornado, but something was looming in the distance. She let the lace curtains fall back closed, as a shiver on the back of her neck unnerved her.

The rain began to fall, and lightning flashed in the distance. Dagmar refused to even acknowledge it any further. "The rain will fall, and the sun will then shine. I don't care," she said. "Harry will come to me soon." After Myrtle died, she had almost forgotten how to dream, but today she was certain, Harry would come. Her heart would soar, and she would fall into his arms, forever and always. It was her destiny.

Chapter 10

Lars Christianson stood at the door of the largest, most ornate house in all of Minaka Falls. Tapping the door knocker, he wondered why he had never been invited to his best friend's home before. They had been buddies for well over a year now and Harry was secretly smitten with Lars' sister, Dagmar. The door opened and a very fragile looking, Mrs. Hanson inched the door partially open.

"I'm sorry, Lars, Harry isn't in," she said.

"Thank you, Mrs. Hanson, but I'm here to see Mr. Hanson. If I may."

Lars stepped inside following Mrs. Hanson to the front parlor, where she quickly disappeared without another word. He was seeing why Harry called it the mausoleum. The furnishings were elaborate and grandiose. No cozy quilts or stitching, like Mamma and the girls make. No pieces of whittled flutes and figurines that he and Papa crafted by the fire at night. This was a cold, lifeless place to live.

"What can I do for you, young man?" Karl Hanson took his

place of prominence in the large leatherback chair.

"I've brought the deeds," Lars said. "Everything should be in order. Papa and Mr. Krog have already put the deposit on the lease for the new dealership and Mr. Gustermen and Papa have settled their arrangement." Lars was proud of his father's determination and accomplishments.

"Ah, very good young man, now let's talk of your future," he said. "I've secured a scholarship for you at the university. Plus, room and board," Karl Hanson said, watching Lars' expression of excitement.

Lars was stunned. He had almost given up hope of ever leaving Minaka Falls, going to university, and with God's help, becoming a doctor. This was his dream, more than he could ever imagine. "How can I ever thank you, sir?" Lars jumped to his feet, attempting to embrace his benefactor, but was stopped abruptly, when Mr. Hanson put his hand in front of him.

"None of that. You're a grown man, now," Karl said.

George appeared at the door. "Sir, there is a phone call for you from grandmother. Will you take it?"

Lars wasn't quite sure what to do with himself after Karl Hanson's abrupt departure from the room, with no explanation or pleasantries. He straightened his neck collar, which was growing more annoying by the minute.

"Hello, Lars," George said shutting the door behind him. "What tangled web does my father have you involved in?"

"It's nothing of that sort," Lars said, not wanting to get between a family squabble. "He has been very kind and generous to me and my family."

"Of course," George said, in a sarcastic tone. "Beware, Lars. My father is neither generous nor kind." The door to the study burst open and Karl returned looking frazzled. George

49

smirked at his discomfort and left the room.

Lars shifted on his feet and reached into his pocket. "Sir, I don't want to take any more of your time, but could you give this note to Harry from my sister when he returns?"

Karl Hanson snatched the envelope and tossed it to the side table. "Certainly, but we have a few details to settle in our arrangement first."

Lars sat down on the chair across from Mr. Hanson uncertain what had made him so agitated, but instantly knew this was not a man to be crossed.

The afternoon had been long and tedious. Dagmar had cleared the noon meal away and had attended to some badly needed housekeeping. Olga's timing was as usual, impeccable, arriving as the last bit of laundry had been pressed and put away.

"You're never going to believe this!" Olga exclaimed in a whirl of giggles and jubilation. "I'm almost certain to be the new Miss Minaka Falls Golden Princess. Carissa told Elsa, and Elsa told Mavis, that Carissa's father, who oversees the judges said I was the prettiest of all the contestants and could sing like an angel. Imagine, I'm the prettiest and an angel," Olga ended in a breathless declaration.

"That's lovely, Olga. Your accomplishments are never ending," Dagmar snipped.

"Well, thank you very much. What's got a burr in your bustle today?" Olga snapped right back.

"I don't have a burr or a bustle, but I'm sorry, it really is lovely. Mamma isn't feeling well, and it's been a long day," Dagmar said.

Lars walked into the living room wrestling with his thoughts and annoyed to hear the sisterly chatter and sparring. Olga looked determined, as always. He looked down and away from Dagmar. Sweat formed across his brow and his chest tightened. He couldn't meet her gaze, not yet. He asked, "Is Papa here? I need to talk to him, and you two need to quit arguing so much."

"No, he's not and we're sorry. It's nothing. Did you see Harry?" Dagmar waited for a reply.

Lars walked to the fireplace and cast his eyes over the miniature portraits of his family that lined the mantel's edge. How much they had all grown and changed since that Christmas. The happy Christmas before Myrtle had died. Those were simpler and carefree times, days of childish innocence. He turned back and looked at Dagmar. "Harry is gone."

"What do you mean, gone?" She sat looking confused. "He can't be gone."

"He has left town and is headed to the university early," Lars took a deep breath feeling like a Judas with his thirty pieces of silver. Dagmar was stunned as he continued, "I'm to join him. I've gotten my scholarship as well and I'll be leaving immediately, as soon as it can be arranged."

"Harry left? You're leaving? I don't understand," Dagmar pleaded for explanation.

Karl Hanson had been perfectly clear and had left Lars with no choice, if he was to be a doctor, this cut would be deep.

"Harry has gone to St. Paul, where his grandmother lives, and he is to be engaged to a longtime acquaintance of their family." The look of hurt on Dagmar's face nearly caused him to cast aside his dreams and opportunities, but Mr. Hanson had made his ultimatums clear, Dagmar and Harry were no more. He

51

would put an end to the scholarship and call Papa's loans in from the bank. The house, the farm, the new dealership, and everything they loved would be gone. He would crush their family with no regrets. George was right. He was caught in Karl Hanson's web with no hope for escape.

"I don't believe it!" Dagmar shouted. Her body swayed and she struggled to remain standing. Tears were welling in her eyes.

"I'm sorry. It's true," Lars said, knowing he had to finish this cruel task. "You had to know he would never marry you. You're just a common store clerk. Your family has no money. People like that don't marry girls like you." He saw the anger and hurt on his sister's face. As much as it pained him to watch, he had no choice. He had to protect his family.

"Harry isn't like that. He's not like his father," Dagmar sobbed.

Olga rushed to her sister's side, but helped Lars make the final stab to Dagmar's heart. "Come now, it will be all right. You weren't pretty enough for a banker's son, but there are lots of other young men who don't really care about that."

Lars turned away glancing at the pictures once more. There were he and his sisters together as one, on the old farmhouse porch, Dagmar was gazing up at him with such admiration. His heart seemed to twist as Dagmar dashed from the room. There was a great deal of darkness and grief now in his destiny and he was uncertain if she would ever forgive him. One thing for certain, he would never forgive himself.

Chapter 11

Regina Parker slammed down the telephone. "That bastard will pay for this," she muttered aloud. Her youngest grandson had arrived just after dawn that morning. Harry somehow came by train and then a private cab, stumbling and bleeding to her door. She knew Karl was a vicious and intimidating man, but this had crossed the line.

Caroline Parker was the only child of Regina and Nathaniel Parker, of the St. Paul Parkers, heiress to a massive fortune. Nathan had been Regina's senior by more than twenty years. They doted on their only child and took pleasure when a youthful, shy Caroline had become smitten with the city's newest, most enterprising young banker. He was charming and attentive, with all the right credentials. It had been a whirlwind courtship, the talk of the town.

First came young George and then his adorable curly-haired, rambunctious little brother, Harry. Caroline appeared content, but Regina had heard gossip and rumors concerning Karl's less than discreet affairs. Five years ago, a bruised and distraught

Caroline came pleading with her parents to help save her husband and family from ruin. The hushed mutterings of shady partnerships and finances were circulating through the private clubs and boardrooms.

The Parkers had stepped in to prevent shame and possible criminal pursuits, but it necessitated certain changes be made, thus the move to Minaka Falls was financed and secured. A hefty investment was certain to guarantee the procurement of position and respectability, even to the least worthy of such blessings.

All the trial and tribulation became further compounded by Nathan's sudden passing. Regina watched with sadness as her only child and grandchildren withdrew into a life devoid of simple respect and happiness. Karl kept tight control over the comings and goings of both Caroline and the boys. If Regina wished to see them, there was usually a generous gift that was expected to follow, a new automobile, furnishings, or such, all at the expense of Caroline's pride and dignity.

For this reason, Regina had insisted on keeping a tight rein on the family finances. She had not denied her daughter or grandchildren, but Karl had yet to prove his worthiness and today Regina would tolerate this bastard no more. It might take her a little time. First, she would make sure Harry recovered and got settled in university, then she would set her trap to free her beloved daughter. She was done with Karl and the world needed to be rid of him.

Dagmar leaned her head against the cold headstone willing

herself to remain steady. Her stomach churned and she fought not to heave the contents of the breakfast she had scarcely nibbled upon. The leaves in the surrounding trees rustled in the wind. "Looks like it will be a cold winter," Dagmar sighed. "The leaves are still plentiful in the trees and the farmers are saying the corn husks are thicker than usual." She pulled her shawl closer around her shoulders.

"I wish you were here, Myrtle. Remember when you taught me to skate and twirl on the ice? We didn't mind cold or snowy days. Lars would pull us for miles on that old sled," she chuckled. "He's left us now, Myrtle. He's gone to university, but writes he is well, and that Harry will marry in the spring." Dagmar rubbed a gentle hand across her belly and continued with her random, confusing thoughts.

"I must tell you something, Myrtle, but first did I tell you Lars wants to be a doctor. I know," she chuckled again. "Remember all those animals he used to save? It took a week for the house to air out after he brought home a family of skunks. He was certain they were kittens." She pondered her sweet memories for a moment, then moved on. "Myrtle, one of the Henderson boys, well they're not really boys anymore," she added.

"Anyway, one of them keeps coming around hinting at wanting to take me to a movie. He's nice enough, but I love Harry and now…, now that I'm to have a baby, it not possible." Dagmar burst into tears and threw herself across her sister's grave. "He said he would never leave me. I love him, Myrtle. I love him. What am I to do?"

Helga stayed back in the distance, giving her daughter time alone with her grief. She had not intended to intrude upon such a private and personal moment, but it was obvious she had been absent from her children's needs too long, leaving them to muddle through on their own.

"Dagmar," she said, kneeling down and placing her hand on her daughter's trembling shoulders. "Hush my dear," she whispered, while guiding her daughter safely into her arms. "Mamma is here. Mamma is here," she repeated, stroking her hair in a gentle motion. She rocked her as she had done when she was a young child, knowing this would take more to soothe than a scraped knee or broken toy.

Helga was tired and worn. Her body struggled to see her through the long days and her legs ached with pain and agony each night, but nothing like the agony she felt at this moment.

"Mamma, I so sorry I've hurt you, but I love him and…"

"Shush," Mamma said, pressing her finger to Dagmar's quivering lips. "We'll figure this out, but you mustn't tell anyone else. These are women's worries and secrets." Mamma rocked her awhile longer.

Hilda, Helga thought. Hilda was her twin sister, her kindred spirit and closest confidant. In times of trouble, they were as one, giving strength and wisdom that only the love of a sister could give. Yes, Hilda would know what to do.

Auntie Hilda warmed the kettle and listened intently. Dagmar cried, Mamma cried, and Dagmar cried again.

"Well now," Hilda said, wiping her hands on her newly embroidered apron and then placing them sternly on her hips. "You'll not be the first nor last young woman caught in such a situation, but we must take care. Your future depends on it, and we must protect you at all costs," she said.

"Whatever you think is best," Mamma nodded in agreement.

"First, I have something for you." Hilda went to the cupboard and opened one of the small drawers. Shuffling through her papers she at last found what she was looking for. "I've been saving this for you. I was going to bring it to Sunday dinner and see what you thought, but this is the perfect plan," Hilda beamed at the thought of her genius.

Dagmar stared at the application. The University of Chicago Secretarial School was printed in large bold letters. She was tired and confused. "What is this?" she asked.

Helga smiled at her sister. "You are the clever one," Helga sat back in her chair and clasped her hands together. "That's the perfect solution."

"Yes," Hilda said. "It is perfect. It's a correspondence course, they say. You don't have to go to the school, but no one else need knows that."

"She can just send her work to them by postal mail. Dagmar is smart. She will do well," Helga said.

"She'll pretend she has gone away for school and training. Hans will need an excellent secretary at the car dealership. I will write Cousin Marvin, in Wisconsin. He and his wife have no children and would be happy to help. It will be for the best!" Hilda exclaimed, and Mamma nodded in agreement.

Dagmar sat listening to the two sisters spinning the details of their master plan, as if she was merely watching through a window, a window to her destiny over which she had no control. Gone were her dreams. Dreams of happiness and Harry were no more. In their place was the reality of shame and despair far away from the family she loved. Far away from Harry.

Chapter 12

agmar's heart pounded with excitement, fear, and dread. She had never been on a train before or even scarily out of Minaka Falls. Mamma and Papa waved from the platform as the train doors slammed, the steam hissed, and the train began to clank and wobble its way down the track. Papa was none the wiser.

"Ticket, please," the conductor with a neatly trimmed mustache and cheerful smile requested. Dagmar smiled back, feeling encouraged by her first encounter with a kind stranger. Thankful for the heat aboard the train, she loosened her jacket while placing her gloves in her satchel. She closed her eyes, hoping to rest for a short while.

Two nights before, her father had seen a snowy owl perched and waiting for its prey. He had explained that the winter would be harsh with their arrival south so early, but they were a sign of good luck and happiness. Dagmar was uncertain whether happiness was destined to be part of her future, but she hoped for better for her child. Seeing no better alternative, she followed along with Auntie Hilda's plan.

Wondering what kind of people her cousin and his wife were, she tried to envision her arrival. She had only met Marvin once a long time ago and remembered him vaguely as being older, awkward and a bit unkempt, but she was certain time and a wife had cured the shortcomings of his youth. In present circumstances, who was she to judge, she reminded herself.

Her mind wandered as the hours toiled on by. Perhaps they lived in a cute little cottage near a lake, surrounded by lilac bushes and roses. There would be a huge spreading maple tree with a dangling swing and sprawling branches to climb. The dock would be long enough to have a small fishing dingy, and Harry could teach their sons and daughters to fish.

Dagmar jerked awake. There would be no dock, no swing or roses and lilacs, but most of all there would be no Harry. She had to come to grips with her circumstances. Her belly was rounding and growing bigger and bigger by the day. She had no husband and no fine little house by the lake.

Perhaps it was as Auntie Hilda said. This was for the best. She closed her eyes and tried to doze off, just for a few moments of peace and to save her dreams for another day, but not today.

The train whistle blew, and the wheels screeched and squealed to a stop. People got off and people got on, each seemed to be certain of their destination and direction, Dagmar envied them and wished she were anyone but herself, a sad, foolish girl. This is for the best, she silently repeated. This is for the best.

"Next stop, Wellings!" the conductor shouted looking less worn by the journey than she. "Five-minute stop. Next stop Wellings, Wisconsin," he repeated before exiting into the next car, leaving a whoosh of frigid air whisking about.

Dagmar gathered her belongings and prepared for her new temporary life in an unknown place surrounded by strangers. "Harry, why did you abandon me?" she mumbled stepping out onto the platform.

There was no mistaking a slightly older, unkempt, and awkward version of Marvin spitting tobacco on the ground before he strolled towards her. Marvin was a distant cousin, a Berge, whose father was one of The Seven. Trucking and hauling were their business and Nils, Marvin's father, had let it be known that his son was quite successful in Wisconsin. Things had not been so bright in Minaka Falls for the young man, but most chalked that up to youthful shenanigans.

Pleasantries were short before Dagmar struggled to position herself in Marvin's rather cluttered, dented, and beat-up truck. Her satchel and a small box of doilies and baked goods for Matilda, Marvin's wife, were tossed into the back end of the truck with little regard. She settled in for the long drive to her new home and did what she could to shut out the stench of whisky and sweat. Her stomach churned, leaving her feeling lightheaded.

"So, your aunt said the guy was rich and ran out on you, sticking you with a kid." Marvin said.

Dagmar gritted her teeth in anger, refusing to acknowledge his crass and insensitive comments, however true they might be. They rode on in silence until the truck veered to the right down a long bumpy path surrounded by a stretch of trees on both sides. The road was barely wide enough for their vehicle and without warning suddenly opened into a vast frost-covered, hilly clearing. A two-story structure, with a leaning porch, stood surrounded by a menagerie of trucks, wagons, and farm equipment which looked to be in various stages of disrepair. There was no lake, no lilac or rose bushes, not even the smallest of trees to hang a swing on. Dagmar willed herself not to sigh, the inside had to be better, she reassured herself.

"Set your belongings there on the bench by the door," Matilda greeted her. "Come in and let's have a look at you, but you'll not be sleeping in my house," she said, crossing her arms sternly in front of her. "You're on the skinny side if I do say so myself. Hope you don't breed a sickly one."

Marvin stood silent as she circled Dagmar for one last look. Matilda continued, "We're descent God-fearing Christians here. You'll be staying out in the old winter work shed, in the north field. There's a deep well, a warm stove, and an outhouse. There's a table, chairs, a bed or two, and I've left you a Bible, since praying and repenting is all you'll be doing this winter. Marvin will take you up there and he'll be picking you up in the morning so you can go buy your own supplies in town. This ain't no hotel here," she said with a huff, indicating the introductions were over and it was time to leave.

Dagmar sat on the tiny bed pushed against the wall. The shed was just that, a shed, a shack or more precisely, a dilapidated hovel of despair and filth. She rose to her feet and with a grand gesture even Olga would have applauded, she announced, "I'm Dagmar Christianson, daughter of Helga and Hans Christianson, I will not live in squalor."

A squirrel screeched in agreement outside the dingy window that denied her even the slightest ray of sunlight. She rolled up her sleeves, as she had seen Mamma do many times before. With a bucket, rags, a broom, and determination, she would bring light and order to her life, at least for the short time. If this were for the best, she would make some adjustments. She had made her bed, and she was certainly going to have to sleep in it now, but first it would be clean. It was the Norwegian way.

Chapter 13

Marvin's truck rumbled and grumbled outside the shed and all the way to town.

"Take your time and make sure you get everything you need," he bellowed. "I'll be at the bar for a little lunch, but don't tell Matilda. She's got a tongue sharper than a straight-edged razor and I'm not in the mood for all that Godly talk," he added.

Glancing up and down the street, he zeroed in on the Wellings General Store and motioned in that direction. They got just about everything down there and it ought to meet all your needs in one sweep. You can wait over on that bench in the park, or I'll leave the truck unlocked for you. Just stay out of trouble and mind your business, or Matilda will have my head," he mumbled before dashing off to the bar.

Dagmar was satisfied with her purchases and had even added a few niceties to boot. Mamma and Auntie Hilda had been generous with their offerings but cautioned the need to be frugal in case of unforeseen troubles.

It was apparent Marvin and Matilda were seeking compensation for their kind and generous assistance in solving her situation. She would need to pay for the chopped wood, use of the shed, her part of gas for trips into town every two weeks, and anything else that may arise.

Dagmar was thankful for her stash of pickled herring, cheeses, and even a loaf of bread Mamma had insisted she take. This morning she had prepared a generous lunch with her remaining sandwiches and the cookies of which Matilda had proven unworthy. A wrapped tin of warm coffee would serve her well with the cool late autumn temperatures settling in. The park it would be, she decided, seeing a cozy bench on the far side offering her a panoramic view of the entire town.

"Hi. Do you mind if I sit here?" The young woman sat on the cold hard bench next to Dagmar, without really waiting for a reply. "Chilly day isn't it?" she chatted on. "I'm Princess Little Dove."

Looking on in wonder, Dagmar couldn't help but notice the women's shining black, almost blue hair, her golden smooth skin, and fierce commanding eyes. Are you really an Indian Princess?" Dagmar asked.

"Of course, I am. Aren't we all princesses? Or at least we ought to be," she chuckled. "All my friends call me Lili," she said, offering a firm handshake.

"Lili it will be," Dagmar responded, sensing she had met her first real friend. "Are you from around here?"

"Let's just say, I'm from here, there, and everywhere. No place in particular. Oh wait, take one of these," Lili handed her a flier.

"Native American Women's Movement," Dagmar read aloud.

"Yup, that's us. Time to let our voices be heard. Did you know with the Indian Citizen Act, my people are now considered citizens, but it doesn't actually give us all the right to vote. Indians are citizens and women can vote, so how come I can't vote? It's outrageous." Lili was waving her hands about, caught up in her own enthusiasm.

Putting her hand to her mouth, Dagmar tried to stifle her laughter. "My goodness, you certainly are sure of yourself."

"If we don't stand up for ourselves, who will?" Lili said, looking confused at why her new friend would think any differently.

"I suppose you're right," Dagmar sighed. "But right now, I think you should have one of my sandwiches and some cookies before you conquer the world."

The new friendship was bonded with the sharing of a simple feast and warm coffee. Lili shared that her real name was Fiona, named after her mother's aunt, who turned her away when her mother died.

"She didn't want me, so I didn't want her name. I was an orphan, so no one really cared who I was. They took me from my father and put me in a different school. It was harsh, but that's life. You can't look back or all you get is a bucket of tears. Better days are coming," she reassured them both.

Dagmar was intrigued by Lili's determination and confidence. She couldn't remember the last time she had felt that way. Harry had made her feel alive again, even though it had been for such a short while. She had never really considered herself weak or helpless, until Myrtle was gone and then Harry. But what did she know? Before those days, she was merely a child protected by her Mamma and Papa, loved, and adored by her family. How she missed that family. Dagmar smiled and decided she liked this woman of determination whose strength seemed infectious and delightful.

"I'm staying at my cousins, Marvin, and Matilda Berge's place. I'm in the little house in the north field. You should visit me sometime," she told her. "I'm pretty much all alone." Dagmar lowered her eyes. "I'm going to have a baby come spring and…"

Lili stopped her, "And you are a beautiful, strong woman, Dagmar. Don't let anyone tell you different, especially not yourself. Remember, don't look back. Just a bucket of tears. Better days are coming. Say it. Better days are coming. Now believe it." Lili leaned in and hugged her.

"Better days are coming," Dagmar whispered trying to believe it herself. "Thank you, Lili," she said.

Lili jumped to her feet. "I'm sorry. I've got to go. Remember, better days." She rushed off.

Tears cascaded down Dagmar's cheeks. She didn't feel like a strong or beautiful woman and now her only friend was gone. There had been a look of fear on her face before she sprinted away more like a panicked deer than a dove.

"What the hell are you doing?" Marvin's words were slurred but emphatic. "I told you to stay out of trouble and mind your manners!" he shouted.

Dagmar had never felt so frightened in her life, as he yanked her up from the bench. She immediately shielded her arms in front of her baby. "I didn't do anything. Please, you're hurting me," she cried as he dragged her to the truck. "I didn't do anything," she pleaded as he shoved her against the truck.

"The hell you didn't!" he yelled, then punched the truck. If Matilda knew you were talking to one of them filthy heathens, you'd be out on your whoring little ass. I don't give a damn about no useless Seven, Masons, or any of that old country mumble jumble. I take care of me, and you best do the same.

Now get in the truck, and keep your mouth shut." Marvin staggered around to the driver's seat, and they soon headed out of town.

Dagmar lit the dim oil lamp and pushed it to the center of the table. The soft hue of the light did little to comfort her. The first night she had been alone and frightened in the dingy surroundings. Her anger had prompted her to name the little shed her den of sin, where she was expected to pray, redeem herself, and no joy or happiness was allowed to exist. She laid her head on the table recounting Marvin's nastiness and rage. Never had she ever heard such unkindness and hatred towards anyone. Dagmar missed her mother, her father, and brother and sister. She was truly alone and uncertain whether she could survive the long, cold months to come. She wasn't strong and there was no beauty here.

"Better days are coming," she said aloud, as she heard a gentle tap on the door.

"It's me, Lili. Hurry. It's cold out here."

Dagmar knew there would be hell to pay if Marvin caught Lili anywhere near the place, but right now she would not look back or look forward. Right now, there was only her, Lili, and her unborn child. She unlatched the door and cast her fears aside, at least for now she would not be all alone.

Chapter 14

E xactly three days after Lili's arrival, an icy wind blew from the north and snow began to fall. By midday the drifts kissed the edges of the windowsills and there was no sign of it stopping.

"Don't worry," Dagmar said. "We have plenty of food and I brought in extra wood." The little black cast-iron stove served to cook as well as heat. They tended and stoked its flames throughout the day and into the night. If they weren't careful, they would surely freeze to death. The wind howled outside, and Dagmar threw another log into the stove, suddenly thankful for the little shed and the old-fashioned stove, but mostly thankful for Lili.

Lili busied herself helping to do whatever she could.

"I need to earn my keep around here," she said as she hauled in another stack of wood. "I'll keep the path to the outhouse clear and a small area out front," Lili said tossing the wood into the small box next to the stove. She warmed her hands next to the fire and then pulled the only other chair out from the table. "What are you doing here?" she asked.

Dagmar hesitated a moment, but there seemed to be no secrets here in the little shed. She chuckled to herself. Lili had Olga's energy, but in a more practical way. She took a deep breath and figured she might as well share the grand plan.

"My Auntie Hilda is by far the cleverest of all my family, not to mention the bossiest. Her plan was for me to be away at secretarial school, so no one would question my being gone. Now I must fill out this application," Dagmar frowned.

"So, what's the problem?" Lili said, snatching the paper away. She scrolled down the page, blank by blank, impressed with the very concise answers and articulate penmanship. "Wow, you are a baby. You finished school when you were fifteen. You're certainly smart enough," she said, before zeroing in on the on the cause of her friend's despair. "Okay, now let's just get this finished up."

"I don't think I'm acc... acceptable," Dagmar sighed, stuttering her words.

"Nonsense," Lili exclaimed. "Let's see, hmmm. Married? No." She checked the box and moved on. "Children? Not yet," she checked no and gave a reassuring chuckle. "Not really a lie. Good moral character? Absolutely," Lili proclaimed. "You're the best person I know. You took me in, fed me, and no one has ever been as kind to me, but you're still doing the dishes tonight. Besides, who are they to judge? Maybe it's time you decide to be who you see yourself as, not what others tell you, you are."

Lili's words were startling. She had always been content to be a daughter, a sister, a good Norwegian girl, as Papa would say. But who was she now and who would she become? All of it seemed so muddled and confusing. Only time would tell, she thought. Yes, secretarial school was a good idea. The baby kicked her back to reality. *I know little one, this won't be easy, but Aunt Lili is right, we can't look back. Aunt Lili,* she thought. *It was nice to have family once again.*

The snow continued to fall, sometimes for days and the hours ticked by. With all of her lessons completed until after the New Year, Dagmar slipped her needle through the cloth Mamma had sent with her. Using a delicate touch to be certain each stitch lay in perfect order; she finished the last of her Christmas gifts. She had already mailed away knitted scarves for Lars and Papa, slippers for Olga, and laced handkerchiefs with the tiniest of roses for Mamma and Auntie Hilda. This gift was for Lili, a fine pillowcase she could take wherever her travels may take her.

They had chopped down a little tree and had enjoyed decorating it with remnants of paper and ribbons, anything they could find scattered about the little room.

When evening came, Dagmar covered the table with a clean blanket and spread evergreen branches in the center with small holly leaves and berries she had found on one of the few sunny days. They ate the last of Mamma's special cookies meant for Matilda, after their evening meal.

"Do you do this every Christmas?" Lili asked, mesmerized by how their dingy, little shed had been transformed into a thing of magic and beauty.

Dagmar laughed. "At home we would have had lamb and fish, breads, cheeses, desserts, and oh so much more. When we were little Papa would read to us. We would dance around the tree holding hands and sing Christmas carols from here and from our homeland. Dagmar sang, Oh Silent Night Holy Night. Tears gathered in her eyes. "I haven't sung since my sister Myrtle died," she whispered at the end. "Myrtle would have liked you," she said, taking Lili's hand.

Lili looked down and remained quiet before she began at a slow steady pace to tell Dagmar of her past. "I have no family. My mother met my father while teaching at an American Indian school. It was sponsored by her church back east. I was told my father was a full-blooded Comanche. He and my mother married in secret. When I was born, my mother named me after her aunt who was also a teacher. My mother died that day, and my father was forced to return to the reservation, having been told neither of us survived. He later disappeared leaving no trace of where he may have gone. My aunt left, not wanting me or the shame my mother and I had brought upon her family." Lili sat silent again. "At the school I was considered defiant and unmanageable. There was no freedom to be me. I was shaped and beaten to be who I was told to be, but now I am who I choose to be," she said with her chin raised high.

"I think you should be my sister," Dagmar declared. "Myrtle would have liked that and well, Olga, hmm, you'll just have to get used to Olga." She had already told her baby, so it was meant to be.

"Tell me about your man. I know of your family, but what of the child's father? Why are you not with him?" she asked.

Dagmar refused to spoil the night with talk of Harry and unfulfilled promises. "That's a story for another night." she said letting Lili know that was her painful past, but there would be other nights to share such secrets.

Lili hugged her new sister and slept peacefully that night but knew her Christmas dream would someday soon fade away, but that was life.

January was bitterly cold, and February wasn't much better, but as March approached, the sun began to shine more often. They had survived the long winter. Dagmar had completed her studies and was growing larger every day as she neared her time. Mamma had warned that first babies had a mind of their own and could come early or late. God would decide.

Lili and Dagmar had settled into a routine. Marvin came every two weeks. Matilda would stop by every other Sunday, after church, to collect the list and money. Before leaving, she would give Dagmar a regurgitation of the Sunday sermon and added a few good harsh lectures and bible verses of her own. She was as predictable as a clock.

"Make sure you put some of that peat moss I gave you in the fire when your time comes. I'll call for the doctor and you'll be just fine. Don't forget, we've been good to you. I want that baby right away and I want you gone the same day. No need to get attached," Miltilda huffed and closed the door behind her.

Lili always hid out back behind the shed during Matilda's visits. Not long after Matilda left, Lili stormed into the room. "Well little sister," she said with a fierce scowl on her face. "How in the world is she part of your family? She hasn't said one kind word to you in all the time I've been here. Are you sure this is what you want to do?"

Dagmar got up and walked to the back door. She turned

and looked Lili straight in the eye. "I don't have a choice and you know that. I've got to pee again, but when I get back, I don't want to talk about it again." A harsh wind rushed past her before she closed the door.

"It's for the best. It's for the best," Dagmar said repeatedly as she gathered some wood from the quickly diminishing pile on her way back. "It's for the best," she said again walking on, until a chilling scream rang out. "Lili!" she screamed.

Chapter 15

L ili had busied herself, first putting away the noonday
dishes, then stoking the fire trying to steady her
temper. It was a curse, a flaw that had plagued her
all of her life. She should have kept her mouth shut, but why
did that nasty Matilda have to be so mean and holy-holy? As far
as she could see, the cousins had done nothing to help Dagmar.
They dumped her in this little shed, took her money and now
we're ready to take her baby. Lili's anger grew ever more. She
couldn't possibly see Matilda raising a precious little child.

"I'll simply have to make Dagmar see this just can't be," she
said aloud, tossing the fire poker aside.

"What can't be?" Marvin snarled as pushed into the room.

The stench of whisky and hate swirled around him and
whisked in with the wind from behind him filling the room
with fear. Lili panicked and sprinted for the back door. She felt
the grip on his hand pulling her hair and body back, dragging
and scraping her across every inch of the floor.

"Let me go!" she shouted, lashing, and kicking at him with

every inch of her strength.

"Matilda said she thought the girl was hiding something up here." He jerked her hair tighter, and Lili stiffened. "I warned her to stay away from the likes of you. You filthy ingens just don't know your place. You think you can come and stay on my land for free? You think you don't have to pay?" In one swift motion he released her hair and his fist plunged into her face, knocking her flat to the floor.

His words slurred, but Lili knew his intentions were clear. Her face and eye throbbed and blood gushed from her nose. She struggled around searching for anything that would stop what was to come.

"You're going to pay now. Ain't nothing free around here." He covered her mouth with one hand and steadied himself with the other as he plunged himself into her. He grunted and groaned, then shouted, "Damn you, bitch!" when Lili had finally grasped onto the fire poker. She struck him once, then twice, but it was of no use, his weight had pinned her firmly beneath him.

Lili screamed. Her body trembled; certain she would die this day. "Help! Help!" She pleaded for what seemed an eternity, until she suddenly heard a thud and Marvin's body went limp. She struggled to push him from her with all her might.

"Oh, my God. I think I've killed him," Dagmar held a cast-iron skillet in her hands. "I heard you scream. I came as fast as I could. It was the only thing I could think of."

Lili stared at her, then wiped the blood away from her eyes. She could feel the swelling in her jaw and winced when a pain shot through her from deep down inside. There would be time to deal with that later. She struggled to rise, then kicked Marvin in the groin. He moaned and passed back out. "Sorry, little sister, the bastard is still alive. We need to get out of here."

Dagmar took Lili's arm over her shoulder, then stopped. "I need to get his keys to the truck." She put Lili into a chair and moved closer to search his pockets. She could hear him breathing and hesitated before she reached deep in his pocket. The keys jingled and he stirred just a little. She held her breath tight and willed her hand steady. Reaching deeper into his pants, she eased the keys out. Jumping to her feet, she snatched her sewing box and all but dragged Lili out the door. "We better hurry. He'll surely kill us if he catches us," Dagmar said, breathing heavily when she felt the first twinge of pain.

"I don't think so. This time, we're ready," Lili said, holding the long sharp bread knife she had taken from the table while Dagmar searched for the keys. She wasn't afraid to use it and would do whatever she had to do to protect her family: Dagmar, and her unborn child.

Despite her injuries, Lili sped away from the little shed, vowing to leave the cruel memory, pain, and ruthlessness of Marvin far behind her, never to be spoken of again.

"Don't look back," she whispered to herself. "Don't look back." They boarded the only train available for the next three days and were happy when the doors slammed, the steam hissed and train clanged first slowly, then faster and faster, taking them far away, as far as the little bit of money in Dagmar's sewing box would take them. For now, they could rest. They were safe.

Dagmar was relieved when Lili closed her eyes in exhaustion and drifted to sleep. People began to come and go aboard the train and she wondered where their lives were taking them. If she was careful, they had enough for one, maybe two nights of lodging, and Lord knows what would become of them after that. Her back had been hurting for hours now and she had been having terrible cramps. She decided to stand and move about while the train was temporarily stopped to replenish its water and coal supplies. She walked forward into the next car and then turned about to amble her way back.

"Dagmar, Dagmar Christianson is that you?" George Hanson, Harry's older brother stood in front of her looking astonished.

The train jerked to a start, and she stumbled into him. He was bigger and had a more mature look than his brother, but he had the same deep dark sparkling hazel eyes and charming smile.

"Hello George." She stepped back, noticing his steady gaze, taking in her obvious condition. Shame and regret that she had promised she would never have run through her.

He smiled and took her arm. "Let me help you to your seat. It's been a while since I've seen you. Are you traveling far?" he asked.

Dagmar was grateful he said nothing of her swollen belly. He was truly a gentleman. She stepped forward and gritted her teeth, while reaching for the seat next to her. An intense pain gripped her body, and she called out to Lili.

"Dagmar, are you okay?" He waited for an answer, then decided to wait no more. George didn't hesitate before lifting her in his arms to carry her to her seat. "I'll get the conductor and see if there is a doctor on board," he said before rushing away.

Dagmar clutched Lili's hand. "Oh God, what I'm to do now, Lili? Something is wrong. It's not time yet. I can't have my baby on the train. I need my mother," she cried out. "Please help me, Lili."

"Hush, now. We'll be fine. We're going to take this one step at a time, but you need to relax and be calm," she said, seeing George and an older gentleman with a doctor's bag coming towards them. "Remember, better days are coming. I promise."

The doctor shooed Lili and George away so he could speak to and examine his patient. It wasn't long before he waved to them to come and join them once again. "It appears your young wife is nearing her time, but not just yet. I suggest you get her home and into bed immediately. I've given her something to calm her, but she needs rest and a good meal." He tipped his hat and said his goodbyes.

Tears rolled down Dagmar's cheeks. "I'm so sorry George. Thank you for not giving me away."

George was a banker. He had seen that look before, embarrassment, fear, and desperation. These girls were in trouble, and he was certain he may be their last hope.

"I think he's right. You're both coming with me. I'm getting off in Duluth and I'll call for a cab. My home isn't a palace, but there are extra rooms, and we'll figure out what's next." He put up his hand when they began to protest. "Everything will be clearer in the morning."

They settled in silence for the remainder of the ride on the train and to his house. He knew he had been right. The girl his brother had defended so fiercely needed his help and help he would. He couldn't help wondering just who the father may be, but he quickly brushed aside any possibility of it being Harry's child. Hell, he's not much more than a child, himself. George knew eighteen was no longer considered a child, but he was barely a man, nonetheless. He cringed when he remembered Dagmar was even younger.

The call for Duluth came and the matters of today seemed

Chapter 15

far more important than the details of yesterday. There was a baby coming, no matter who the father was.

Chapter 16

The freezing rain pelted against the kitchen window-pane, as Lili stretched and yawned. Her body and mind ached from Marvin's attack, but she couldn't and wouldn't deal with that now. "Good morning," she said as George made his way to the stove for a hot cup of coffee. "I hope it was okay, I made some fresh biscuits from what I could find in your kitchen."

George sat down beside her at the table, thankful he was not left to his own bachelor devices. "Make yourself at home. My housekeeper comes once a week. She wasn't expecting me back until next week, but plans changed," he said.

That was an understatement, he thought. Dagmar and Lili had already been in his home for just over a week. They both slept for most of the first three days. Dagmar was on strict bed rest orders from the doctor George had insisted on calling immediately upon their arrival. Lili moved about the house dusting and cleaning, insisting she would earn their keep.

Neither had been an imposition or burden, but it was time

for George to ask what their plans were. He knew nothing of Lili's background, but what little he knew of the Christianson family, he had greatly admired. They were honest hardworking people who had suffered the loss of their oldest daughter. His brother at one time had been smitten with young Dagmar, but Harry's likes and dislikes were as changeable as the wind. He blamed his father who for some reason took pleasure in belittling and antagonizing Harry at every turn.

"So, Lili, I want you to feel at home here. The two of you need to rest and when you are ready, we can discuss your situation and what I can do to help you both." George took a hearty bite into one of the delicious biscuits and smiled.

"I'm sorry George, I don't really know you, nor you I. But if you did, you would know I speak my mind."

"I respect that in a person," George said before finishing off the last of his biscuit.

"Good, I think you should marry Dagmar."

George's eyes widened in shock and dismay. He coughed and struggled not to choke as he swallowed the last of his breakfast. "I'm sorry Lili, but that's not possible. I don't even know Dagmar and what of the child's father?" He wiped away the sweat forming across his brow.

"There is no father. She loved him, but he is to be married to another. Dagmar is a good woman who is kind and caring," Lili said.

"I'm sure she is, but surely you can't expect me to. I mean I'll be good to my word to help, but I'm not marrying anyone. I'm sorry." George straightened in his chair, wondering how exactly he had gotten himself into this mess.

"Dagmar was sent to her cousins, who were to take the child as their own, but that was a terrible place and we had to leave.

They weren't fit to raise dogs, let alone a precious child. She took me in for the winter and helped me, even though she had little of her own. I will do whatever I can to see her safe and happy," Lili said, tilting her chin high.

It was then for the first time that George noticed the bruises to Lili's face and neck. She had carefully kept them hidden until now, not to draw attention to herself. George couldn't help but admire the concern and loyalty she had for her Dagmar, while ignoring her own obvious wounds. "I promise we'll figure this out. What about adoption agencies?"

"No." Lili slammed her hand on the table. "You don't know where the child would go or what kind of people would care for it. I was raised in an orphanage, and there has to be another way," she pleaded.

"Okay, okay," George said. "We'll figure this out, but I'm not getting married."

"Too bad for you Georgie." Lili said. "She's going to be an amazing woman one day."

George said nothing. He rose from the table and decided it was best if he perhaps went to work at the bank. Clearing his head and getting some perspective on this matter might help. He chuckled to himself. No one except his grandmother ever called him Georgie. He shook his head and smiled, these two were both amazing, strong women and they were worming their way into his heart. Surely, he could find a solution.

Married, he thought. That's crazy, she doesn't even know me. For the life of him, he couldn't believe the whole idea seemed less shocking than it did just ten minutes ago. He definitely needed to go to work and clear whatever stable mind he had left. Married, he thought again. Crazy.

Dagmar straightened the covers on the bed. The days and

hours she had spent resting had given her needed strength and she resolved to focus on what needed to be done.

"It's for the best," she mumbled repeatedly as she fought back her tears. In the dark hours of night, she turned on the small table lamp next to her bed. Taking pen and pad from the same table, she began to write.

My dearest darling,

I want you to know you are loved. Although I was not able to keep you to treasure as my own, I will always love you. Please be happy and well.

Love, your mother,
Dagmar Christianson.

She couldn't say why, she knew it was foolish, but she had been certain from the very beginning, the baby would be a girl. She wasn't sure what her first name would be, but Louisa from Mamma and Myrtle would be her second name as well. She tucked Myrtle's locket in the envelope. It had been her most treasured possession and she wanted her daughter to have it. Oh God, my daughter, she thought. The baby kicked.

"It's for the best my darling," she whispered between her anguished sobs. She had no choice. Her child would go to an agency, and she would return home. It was for the best.

Two days later George had urgently been summoned by messenger to return home immediately. Marta Louisa Christianson was born just after two in the afternoon. Dagmar held her daughter close. She had Myrtle's eyes and Olga's and Lars's curly hair. She prayed she would be kind and gentle like

Mamma and have Papa's integrity and courage. She kissed her daughter's cheek and sang a soft lullaby as Marta's eyes closed. "Sleep my sweet darling. Mamma must make a new plan."

Chapter 17

The chime on his grandmother's old clock on the mantel over the front parlor fireplace told George it was exactly 2 a.m. He chuckled. No need for clocks around here, he thought. Little Miss Marta was wide awake not long ago for a nightly feeding.

Funny, he didn't feel tired at all. It comforted him to know she was in the next room over, nestled in her mother's arms, safe and warm. He was becoming accustomed to the tiny cries in the night, followed by Dagmar's hushed lullabies. Her voice was beautiful and calming. He remembered back what seemed like a lifetime ago when she sang at the church bazaar. She was a child then, but this was a woman's voice, full of joy and love. She had been through so much. He shuddered to think what would have become of them had he not come upon them on that train. It was destiny, and he was sure of it now.

He closed his eyes trying to shut out the reality of the situation. They would all be leaving soon. George had struggled with his thoughts over the past several weeks. His own childhood had been marred by his father's constant drinking, verbal, and often physical abuse. Sadly, his mother and brother had borne the brunt of his father's rage. He was determined never to marry unless he could truly love and honor his wife and family, with the same love his grandparents had once shared.

George worked hard to advance his career, but often wondered if it would be better to have a small house, with a loving wife, surrounded by his children, friends, and community. He frowned thinking that that was what the Christiansons had, but even they struggled for happiness. How they must miss their daughter and how terrible it would be for them to never know Marta. It was settled. He would speak to Dagmar, but first he'd get the needed paperwork and settle a few other details, like getting her a ring. He was certain she'd be her usual stubborn self, but she would have to see, it was for the best.

Dagmar and Marta were growing stronger every day. She wasn't sure how she would ever thank George for all he had done for them and Lili, but it was time to go. She had made up her mind. Dagmar would ask George for a modest loan or ask Mamma and Auntie Hilda, just to get the three of them started. She would find a job, while Lili took care of Marta during the day.

With her completed certificate, Dagmar could earn enough money for them to live frugally, but safely and together. She had taught Lili how to stitch and mend over the long winter.

Maybe they could earn extra money that way and pay George back quickly. Somehow, they would manage until Marta was school age. Dagmar gave a cheerful sigh, thinking of a young curly haired Marta off to school.

"This is for the best," she said aloud to little Marta. "I'll have to talk to Auntie Lili. We won't be going back to Minaka Falls. I'm sorry you won't know our family, but it would be too difficult for us both. We will stay here in Duluth and maybe Uncle George will help find me a job," she said, then tried to shutter her thoughts.

She couldn't possibly tell George the truth about her and Harry, but if she was careful, Marta could still know her uncle, an uncle who seemed to love her more every day. First, she would look for a job, then she would tell Lili and George her plan. They would miss what they had all shared here.

George was a kind and loving man, and she would miss that very much, Dagmar thought. She had grown very fond of him, she had to admit, and blushed when her thoughts deepened. Shaking her head, she then looked back at her sleeping daughter.

"Sorry, Mamma was being silly. It's just us girls now, and we're going to be fine." Mamma, she thought. I'm a Mamma and I'm going to take good care of you.

Standing across the street from the bank, Dagmar glanced into the window of the Woolworth's 5 & 10. A small sign caught her eye, and she began reading aloud, "Help wanted, part-time accounting, apply inside." Perfect, she thought. She straightened her dress and hair in the window and froze, petrified at what she saw.

"Hello, little cousin. Nice to see you again," Marvin said. "Thought you got away, didn't you?"

Dagmar couldn't move. She wasn't sure if the pungent smell of his filth and whiskey or just plain fear would do her in first. She suddenly thought of how he had savagely beaten Lili and she willed herself to run.

Run. Run. I have to protect Marta, she thought, as her feet pounded against the pavement. Please God, don't let him catch me, was her last thought before she felt herself being tossed into the wall in an alleyway. Her heart raced as she tried to shield herself when she saw his fist above her.

"You and that half-breed think you can cheat me," he growled into her face. "Matilda wants that baby, and we want it now."

The hold he had on Dagmar suddenly released and Marvin went sprawling to the ground. George grabbed him by the shirt and landed another solid punch to his jaw. Marvin yelped in pain.

"Stay away from my wife and my daughter or I'll kill you," he said pulling Dagmar to him, then walking as fast as they could down the street.

They stopped at the park bench several blocks away when they were certain Marvin had not followed. Dagmar laid her head on George's chest, shivering in fear.

"I'm so sorry, George. I thought he was going to kill me and take Marta away. I'm so sorry. I've made such a mess," she said as the sobs continued.

George was calm. He had a plan and now he knew she needed his protection more than ever. "It's okay. He can't hurt you. I'll protect you, but I must know one thing. Is he Marta's father?"

"No," Dagmar said, shaking her head. "Never. He's an awful, horrible man and my cousin. I stayed at their place in the winter and…"

"It's okay. Lili told me some," he said, pulling her closer.

George stroked her back trying to calm her, smelling his soap in her hair. He would have to do better than that, he thought. He kissed her on the top of her head and pledged to buy her lavender, roses, peaches, and gardenia soap. Whatever she wanted. He would take care of her now and forever.

"Dagmar, now that you are my wife…"

"I'm so sorry you had to lie. I promise we'll leave right away. I'm so sorry," she sighed.

"That's just it," he paused. "I don't want you to leave. I don't want Marta to leave, and I've even gotten used to Lili. I want you to marry me and I'll be Marta's father. You'll be safe and all these problems will go away. I was going to talk to you tonight but saw that man chasing you from the bank window. It would solve everything. You'll be safe and no one will take Marta away." He sat waiting for her response.

Dagmar shut her eyes in a swirl of confusion. She thought of her family, Mamma, Papa, Auntie Hilda, her siblings, Lili, and even Harry. No, she thought. Harry abandoned me and Mamma and Auntie Hilda meant well, but only George can help me keep my daughter. I must take care of Marta.

"Yes, I'll marry you George, but first you need to know, I love another. He doesn't love me, but I will always love him. I'll be a good wife, but I don't want to lie to you," she said, certain he would cast her away.

"I will accept that, Dagmar. You're honest and loyal. I would expect no less when you've given your heart to someone. I hope one day you will grow to love me as well. I've all the paperwork here in my coat pocket and a ring I hope you will like. I think we should marry today to be certain your cousin bothers you no more. I think it's for the best," he said smiling to reassure her all was well.

Two hours later Dagmar opened the front door as Mrs. George Hanson. She was safe. Marta and Lili were safe. She was very fond of George and would learn to love him. She had been honest with him, except for the one secret she could never tell him or anyone else. Marta would be his daughter now and no one could ever change that.

The house was quiet. "Lili, we're home," she shouted, but no one answered. She saw a letter leaning against the lamp on the entryway table. Dagmar opened it and began to read. Her hand went to her chest. "She's gone! My Marta is gone!" she screamed as she fainted to the floor. Marta was gone.

Chapter 18

L ars pulled his jacket tightly around himself. The chill of winter had not quite left the shores of Lake Superior. Duluth was a growing, prospering shipping city, connecting goods from the eastern ports westward. He looked out over the water and wondered how far Harry had gotten on his journey. The weather had been rough, and Lars tried to get Harry to wait until the storm passed and perhaps go with him to see his brother, George, but Harry would have none of it.

Lars had phoned ahead, telling George that he would be arriving this morning only for a few days. He wanted to see Dagmar and speak to George personally. There was no turning back. The lies and manipulation had gone too far, and he had to set some things right. Harry was gone and lost to them all, for how long he did not know. George and Dagmar deserved the truth, no matter what it cost him. He quickened his step across the street and into the bank.

George had a small office close to the front and rushed to

greet him. "Hello, Lars. How are you?" George's handshake was firm and welcoming. "Did Harry come with you?" he asked, now looking a bit concerned.

"Can we go somewhere quiet?" Lars asked.

"Yes, of course. Come into my office. George offered Lars a chair and remained standing looking more and more worried. "Is my brother all right?"

"That's why I've come to see you. Harry has quit school and I have no idea where he has gone." Lars said.

"Damn that brother of mine," George huffed in annoyance rather than concern. "Did my dear brother give any reason for this sudden departure, or was it just too much work for the likes of him?" He pulled out his chair and sat before pounding his fist on the desk.

Lars studied George's reaction carefully but saw no other way out. He couldn't play this crazy game Karl Hanson had set him up in any longer. If he lost his scholarship, he would just have to find a different way to finish his credentials. George had a right to know why his brother had sworn never to return to Minnesota and never to see his father again.

"Well?" George said tapping and fidgeting with a pencil on his desk. "You were his best friend. You must know something. Damn that brother of mine," George repeated.

"It's not all Harry's fault," Lars began before he laid out the details of how Karl had been furious when Harry and Dagmar had first started seeing each other in secret. He told him how his father, Hans, had gotten a loan to start the new dealership from Karl at the bank. "Then Karl secured a scholarship for me," Lars continued. "When everything was set, he called me in and told me he would call in my father's loans and see to it that my scholarship was canceled. He threatened to ruin my family and my sister. I had no choice, but to do as he told me to do." Lars sighed.

"What did he tell you to do?" George's jaw was clenched, and his hand had broken the pencil in half.

Lars wiped the sweat from his brow, there was no turning back.

"I told Dagmar Harry was engaged and in love with a friend of your family." He lowered his head between his hands and continued in shame. "I kept Harry's letters I was supposed to give to Dagmar and then told him she was seeing someone else. We got drunk one night, and I told him you and Dagmar had married. He was furious, and it was then that I knew I had betrayed my best friend and my sister. I told him the truth." Lars paused, uncertain how George would react.

"I can't believe this. How could you do this to your sister?" George groaned. "Never mind, I know exactly why you did it. My father is a manipulating bastard who would have had no problem doing exactly what he said he would. But did you even stop to think about the baby?" George stopped when he saw the look of astonishment on Lars's face. "Yes, there was a baby," he said, then shared the tale of Dagmar's despair. "I think it's best if you leave and not see Dagmar. I'm not sure she needs to know all this right now. You're her brother, you know how the loss of Myrtle hurt her, then Harry, her friend Lili, and her daughter."

"My God, she had a daughter?" Lars mumbled, choking back his tears. "What have I done?"

"Go back to school and become a doctor," George said. "I'll handle my father. He'll never know we have spoken. For now, let your sister be in peace."

Lars left knowing George was wrestling between his anger

for his father and his love for Dagmar. He knew George would protect his sister, and he prayed maybe that love would be enough to make up for the loss of her daughter. He also prayed that she would one day forgive him but knew that forgiveness would not come easy.

The old clock chimed, chimed again and again every hour. The days and nights dragged by with no word of Lili and Marta. Dagmar sat by the big bay window waiting, praying for news to come. Lili's letter, now creased, worn, and tear stained lay folded in her lap.

My Dear Dagmar,

Please forgive me for what I am about to do. You are the kindest and only friend I have ever had. You have struggled for so long and I can't bear it any longer. I know you have gone to speak with the agency today. I can't let you do this. It will break your heart forever. I told you I was an orphan and don't want Marta to carry the same life. I promise you I will care for and love her as my own. I've gone to seek my mother's family back east. I love you. Now go have the life you deserve with your family.

Love, Lili

Dagmar no longer needed to read the words. Each line was etched on her broken heart. She should have told Lili of her plans, and this never would have happened. Lili meant well, just like when Mamma and Auntie sent her to Cousin Marvin's and when George talked her into marrying him. This was all her fault.

The only decision Dagmar had ever made on her own was to be with Harry, which now seemed a million years ago. No, she would not regret that, ever. She had a beautiful daughter from their love, if only for a short while. She would not give up hope, never.

George had hired a private detective agency to search for Lili and Marta, but there were few clues. Dagmar wasn't even sure what Lili's true name was or where her mother's family came from. They chased one dead end after another, by the trains and buses. There had even been a man who claimed to have driven them near St. Paul, but that too was untrue. Lili had simply disappeared and young Marta with her.

The motion of everyday life pushed forward. Dagmar had written to Mamma and Papa telling them of her good fortune to have completed her certificate but would not be returning to Minaka Falls. She was now Mrs. George Hanson of Duluth.

Ours is a fine home and we hope to bless you with grandchildren one day. All is well and as it should be; she wrote. She hoped Mamma and Auntie Hilda would rest easy now. It was for the best they didn't know all the details.

Grandchildren, she thought. How could she possibly even think of it? But she had promised George she would be a good and faithful wife. He was a kind man who had tried his best to protect and comfort her. He had been patient with her after they married, never asking, or demanding her affections, but tonight that would change. She would be what George deserved.

Chapter 19

George stumbled home that night, wrapped in anger, confusion and an intoxication that would surely cost him in the morning. His bastard father had once again set his family up for more pain and disaster. It wasn't bad enough his mother put up with the constant verbal and physical abuse, his brother would now be denied the woman he loved and, if George wasn't mistaken, his child as well.

George felt a tightness across his chest and the beginning of a throbbing headache. Not only would his brother lose the woman he loved, but God help him, George had to face the reality, he loved Dagmar and would never let her go, not even for his brother.

His wife intrigued, excited, and soothed him in so many ways. Harry and Lili were right, she was an amazing woman. Although neither had spoken any words of love, he prayed once they had come together and known each other as husband and wife, maybe then this marriage based on good intentions and guarded secrets might grow. He would make her happy, and he would find Marta, but tonight, he needed to climb the stairs and find his bed. Maybe she wouldn't notice the state he was in and give her one more reason to doubt this marriage and cling to her broken promises of a love now lost. He would have to do better tomorrow, he thought.

Already dressed in her nightgown, Dagmar had settled in for the night. George called to let her know he was working late. She wasn't the least surprised as the hours ticked away. The streetcar union had gone on strike and other protests were occurring throughout the city.

George was growing more and more concerned about the economic soundness of the bank and the country at large. It was part of one of the many conversations they shared each evening. Dagmar appreciated how compassionate he was to those who were struggling and how he encouraged her to speak her mind on the various events going on around them.

She missed that tonight as she slid into the large, lonely bed, the bed they slept in, but were yet to truly share as man and wife.

The hours ticked by, and Dagmar grew concerned. She got up and nestled herself on the chaise chair in the corner of the room near the window. The moonlight cast a faint flickering of light and she could feel the coolness of the night on the windowpane. Dagmar didn't enjoy being alone at night. There had always been her family, especially Myrtle, who she had never been apart from until she was gone. Then Lili had blessed her during that dark, agonizing winter before Marta was born. Now, George had come to her rescue. But where was he now, she thought.

"Myrtle!" she cried aloud. "Why did you leave me? I need you now, more than ever." Dagmar drew her knees to her chest as the tears fell. She was so confused and the quiet of the night magnified her fears and doubts.

Myrtle, I'm so alone, she thought. I miss you so much. Everything is such a mess. My Marta is gone, Harry is most likely married to someone else and poor George married me to save me and I'm a terrible wife. He's so kind and caring and now he's stuck with me. I've ruined his life and worst of all I've lied to him. I can't ever tell him. He would never forgive me.

"He's a good man, Myrtle," she whispered as she heard the front door close, and George finally climb the stairs to their bedroom just after midnight. She squeezed her eyes shut and tried to dry her tears. This was the last thing her husband needed, a weak, sniveling, and completely useless wife. God, what a mess she had made. She sat quietly in the dark as he changed into his robe and crossed the room where he sprawled across the middle of the bed on his back as if she weren't even there. If it were only true, his life would be so much better, she admonished herself once again.

Grabbing the quilted blanket from the chaise, she thought it was the least she could do to cover him from the night air. She stopped at the edge of the bed and perused where his robe had fallen to the side. Heat rose deep inside her as her eyes caught the first glimpse of him and the carved muscles of his abdomen. Her mouth went dry, and her fingers itched to touch and roam through the thick dark hair on his chest. Dagmar clutched the blanket close as he stirred again.

George moaned and stretched his body to get comfortable, shifting his robe further. She reached her hand down to pull it back in place, then froze.

His eyes were wide open, sharp, and steady, filled with

yearning and desire. He yanked her closer into his arms, claiming her with a long passionate kiss before she had a chance to pull back or protest. "I want you, Dagmar. I need you."

Dagmar's body melted at the flavor and softness of his lips, as his hands reached beneath her nightdress up her bare legs, sparking her passion inch by inch. Aching for his touch, she gasped as he sought her breasts, kneading her flesh and massaging her nipples beneath his thumbs.

"I'm sorry I've been so foolish," Dagmar whispered as he trailed his kisses across her body, weaving a web of pleasure.

"Shush," he pleaded. "Let's have no apologies or regrets between us tonight," he said, then ravished her mouth once again, as he entered her, and they sealed their vows as husband and wife.

Both slept a blissful sleep, cocooned in one another's arms, each willing to push away their doubts, fears, and secrets, at least for tonight. Night would become day soon enough to weather what had been and what will become their destiny together.

Chapter 20

T he sun had nearly pushed the darkness away as George cradled his sleeping wife in his arms. He listened to her soft easy snore and wanted to stop time forever. She had been through so much in such a short time in her life. He just wanted to hold her and protect her from all the pain of her past and what was sure to come once he told her of his father's manipulation and cruelty. He prayed she would forgive his family and understand he had no part in it. But there had been enough secrets and unspoken words. Dagmar deserved the truth, but he would regret nothing. He would fight for her, for them. She was his family now and prayed she loved him enough to stay.

Dagmar remained still, like an angel in his arms when he heard a loud knocking downstairs on the front door. Easing her onto the pillow, he quietly pulled the covers back over her and snatched the pants he had discarded to the floor the night before. George crept down the stairs and was stunned to see a very distraught Lars on his front steps.

Chapter 20

"What's wrong?" he said, pulling him inside. Lars stood silent until George repeated himself. "Tell me. What's wrong?"

"Harry is missing."

"What do you mean, missing?" he said, shutting the door behind them.

"I told him not to go, that the weather was too rough. He just wouldn't listen. I begged him. He just wouldn't listen."

Lars was visibly shaken, and George could feel his concern. "Calm down, Lars," George said as much to himself as Lars.

"You don't understand, George. The boat Harry was on two nights ago sank and he isn't among the survivors. There's no sign of him and they think he must have drowned."

George stepped back, bracing himself against the wall. "My God," he said as he heard Dagmar gasp in shock and then watched her sink to her knees at the top of the stairs clinging to the wooden banister.

"Dagmar," George shouted taking the steps two at a time. "Dagmar, my love," was all he could think to say rocking her in his arms before lifting her limp body. He carried her back to their bed, where only hours ago they had slept in such passion and peace. Now, everything had changed.

Lars left without even seeing his sister. George had done his best to assure him he would take good care of her, and they would leave for Minaka Falls immediately.

"She's had a great shock and we're going to have to give her time to sort it out," he told Lars with a final goodbye.

George gathered himself, making the necessary phone call to his grandmother. It had been agreed she would be present when he informed his parents of the tragic news, Harry was gone. He tried to push his thoughts aside as he packed their belongings in a small suitcase and guided a numb and lifeless

Dagmar to the car. They meandered on the back roads to Minaka Falls as the hours ticked by. George agonized, watching her stare out the window without saying a word.

"We'll be there soon," he said. "We need to see my parents first, then I will take you to see your family. My grandmother will meet us there." He wasn't quite sure if she even heard what he said. Gone was the gentle peace he saw in the early morning as she rested in his arms. This would be yet one more layer of pain for her to bear.

His pain and that of his family were yet to come. Just a few more miles and he would deal with that. His grandmother, despite her age, was strong and would comfort his mother. His father, well he couldn't think about him right now. He really didn't deserve his sympathy or concern, anyway. He had to put the bastard out of his mind and focus on the road ahead.

"It was Harry," Dagmar whispered.

"It's okay, my love. We'll figure this out," George said.

"You don't understand. It was Harry that I loved, and he was Marta's father," she whispered.

"I know. I guess I've always known," George said and reached to place one hand on her leg until she turned and stared out the window. The pain was unbearable, but he knew there was more to come. Minaka Falls lay just ahead.

Dagmar remained silent as she took George's hand when he rushed to open the car door. Always the kindest, even in his own grief, she thought. She would have to try harder to be the wife he deserved. Harry was gone and most likely Marta forever. She needed to be stronger and support him as he delivered the most awful news a family could hear, losing a child.

Harry wasn't a child anymore, she thought, but he had barely grown into a man, the last time she saw him. She searched her memory, desperate to recall every minute they spent together and try to etch it in her heart. Their time had been short, filled with an overwhelming need to comfort one another. She had never been to his home, met his parents, or mingled among his friends. Dagmar felt an ache in her chest. She closed her eyes; aware she was mourning what may have been. Had they really spent so little time together? She loved Harry. She had been certain of it, but she struggled with the confusion of her fading memories. Dagmar stopped abruptly at the front door and turned to George.

"I thought Harry was getting married. Why was he even on that boat? I don't understand," she said. She waited for George to answer. Something wasn't right, here. Before she could ask again, the front door opened and Caroline, looking older and smaller than Dagmar recalled, ushered them in. But she was certain George wasn't telling her something.

They were welcomed into the front parlor and Dagmar felt more and more uneasy for both her and her husband.

George paced the room looking more and angry with each step. "Where the hell is he? Grandmother told me you called him over an hour ago to come home. Why do you put up with him?" George scowled as he moved about the room before standing next to his wife.

"George," Regina said. "Let's not air our dirty laundry in public, please."

"We're not in public, grandmother. Dagmar is my wife and I demand she be treated respectfully."

"I'm so sorry," Caroline said looking embarrassed and ashamed. "I'm sure he'll be here soon."

"Don't apologize for me. This is my house and I'll damn well get here when I please," Karl snarled, tossing his belongings on the chair. "So, you brought your little storekeeper wife home. Couldn't be bothered to include your mother and I in the wedding, so don't expect me to jump to your demands now," he said pouring himself a whiskey at from the crystal decanter kept on the side table next to the chair he now claimed.

Harry's descriptions of his father were standing in front of Dagmar. She gritted her teeth thinking, this is a hideous man. Sadness overwhelmed her for Caroline. She rested her hand on George's arm as he stood next to her, looking as if he wanted to pounce on his father.

George looked at his mother and to his grandmother and placed his hand on his wife's slender fingers. He took a deep breath and sighed. "I've not come here to argue with you. We had planned to visit soon, but bad news has brought us here today."

The room went silent until Karl all but shouted, "Spit it out then! I've got things to do."

Dagmar admired how George ignored his father's rudeness and continued with the agony of the task ahead.

"Harry is missing. He was on a boat going east across Lake Superior. The weather was rough, and he is presumed dead." George squeezed Dagmar's hand and watched his grandmother put her arms around his mother. "I'm so sorry," he said.

Moments passed before Karl poured himself another drink. He gulped it down then tossed the glass at the fireplace.

"What the hell was he doing on a boat? You wasted your money on that one, Regina. He was a Mamma's boy idiot. No loss there." Karl said getting up to leave the room.

Dagmar sat in shock as George lunged for Karl. He grabbed him by the shoulder, turning him quickly and pushing him back against the wall.

"You killed him, you bastard!" George screamed. "You picked at him all his life! You pushed him and dared him every inch of his life. That wasn't enough. Not nearly enough, and you threatened and manipulated Dagmar's family. You beat him and sent him away, robbing him of the woman he loved and his daughter. You're a worthless bastard," George raged on. He raised his fist, prepared to strike his father.

Caroline screamed as Karl fell back to the floor. He stood with his hands still balled above his father when Regina shook him. "You must call the doctor. He's had a stroke," she said.

George turned to go to the phone in the front hallway, as he watched Dagmar close the front door behind her, leaving him without a word.

"I hope she hasn't left you for good, but who would blame her for leaving this family?" Regina went back into the parlor to wait for the doctor and mumbled prayers for Karl's early departure. "God help us. God help us all."

Chapter 21

K arl was carried upstairs.

"The damage is done," Dr. Jenson said. "All we can do now is let him rest and pray he comes out of it, then we will know where we stand. I've done all I can. It's in God's hands now." He gave his farewells and quietly left the house.

The curtains were drawn, and the room remained in a dreary darkness. Caroline had slipped away on Regina's insistence to rest while she could.

"Your mother needs our prayers and some rest right now. The doctor is right, Karl is in God's hands. May His will be done," his grandmother said before leaving the room.

George sat in a wing-backed chair steps away from his father. "You've really done it now Father," he whispered into the faint darkness. "Harry is gone, Mother is devastated, and you've finally driven Dagmar away. Are you happy, Father? Are you happy?"

George sighed, leaning forward, and resting his head between his hands. Closing his eyes, he tried to imagine what he could say to Dagmar to get her to return to him. Was it even possible? He had allowed his father's vicious words to rile him and lost control. He had done exactly what he had spent a lifetime telling his little brother not to do. No one challenged Karl and won, but today the remnants of Karl's destruction lay all around, cloistered in every room of the most expensive, ornate, loveless house in Minaka Falls. When Dagmar closed the door and hadn't said a word or even bothered to look back, he knew she would never forgive him.

The distance to her parents' home was less than ten blocks from the Hanson house, but they were a world apart. No fancy furniture or imported rugs adorned their home, just a little of this and that, but a lot of love. Dagmar had never heard her papa raise his voice or speak harshly to her mamma. Her parents cherished each of their children, especially after Myrtle died so suddenly.

Myrtle, she thought, as she stood in front of the church, next to the cemetery. She smiled. Myrtle will know what to do. Through the side gate and around the back, she followed the neatly groomed pathway. There was Mamma, sitting on a little stool Papa had made for her to get up and down in her garden. Sitting and kneeling on the ground had become such a struggle for her.

"Dagmar," she called.

"Mamma, what are you doing here by yourself?"

"Oh nonsense," Mamma said. "Olga is at choir practice and

will help me home later. Lars told Papa you were coming, and I wanted to have a little visit before you got here."

Dagmar sat down on the grass next to Mamma and whispered a brief prayer to Myrtle.

"Tell us what's bothering you, my sweet one. Myrtle and I are listening."

There was no hiding any secrets from Mamma or Myrtle. Mamma always said that twins, especially sisters, have a special magic to know when one is in trouble or full of worry. She and Auntie Hilda had that magic. She once told her that a mother's magic is even stronger.

Dagmar sighed and began her tale from the very beginning. She told her about Lili and the cruelty of Cousin Marvin and his wife. How George had rescued them from the train and married her, trying to save her and her daughter.

"A daughter," Mamma gasped holding her hand to her heart. "I'm so sorry, Dagmar. I thought they would be good to the child. I'm so sorry." She bowed her head down as tears and remorse consumed her. "Where is the child now?"

Dagmar continued the story of Marta's disappearance and how Lili thought she was protecting them both. How George had searched for them but found nothing. She told her of Karl's cruelty and deception. How he had manipulated Lars and threatened to ruin Papa all to keep her and Harry apart.

"He's a horrible man and now he's had a stroke and may die," Dagmar said.

Mamma brushed her tears away and raised her chin high. "Why are you not beside your husband?" There was a sternness in her eyes.

"He lied to me. He knew about Harry all along and..."

Mamma raised her hand for Dagmar to stop. "You do not

108

know that. You are not a child any longer. You must speak to your husband and find out the truth, but first ask yourself if you, too, have been truthful with him. Lies do not make for a good marriage. You've told me that he is a good man and if there is any possibility you are with child, you must trust him and trust yourself to see if this is your destiny."

Dagmar was in shock. Oh my God, could this possibly be true? She had only slept with George once, but it had been the same with Harry. This just could not be happening again. But her mother was right. She needed to speak with George. She at least owed him that and then she would decide what to do, but it would be she who decided this time, and no one else.

From the moment Dagmar returned to the Hanson house, she felt the weight of its despair. A shiver ran up her spine. How could love and joy grow in a home of such twisted anger and abuse? She felt for those who had endured such pains. She questioned who these people were and who was this man she had married. Climbing the steps, one by one, she realized, for better or worse, they too were her family now.

The threads of her sins and shame had been shouted about for all to hear. Dagmar entered the room, the Hanson abyss of hate and anger. There were no secrets here, but she would not have the details of her life discussed in the open again. What was between her and George would have to wait. For now, she would stand by her husband's side.

"Dagmar," Regina said looking relieved to see her. Caroline sat beside her, rubbing her hands endlessly together, while staring straight ahead as if wrapped in a tomb of endless sadness.

George got up from the chair and moved to the doorway to welcome his wife. "I'm so sorry. Please let me explain," he pleaded.

"We'll speak later," Dagmar said, taking her husband's hand to reassure him that she was going nowhere. "How is your father?"

He pulled her aside. "There's been no change. We're just sitting here waiting to see if he wakes up or not. Mother is distraught, and grandmother is angry." He touched her cheek and said, "I really am sorry."

Dagmar's own anger was beginning to wane. George wasn't like his father. He was kind and gentle.

George suddenly pushed her aside and dashed to the bed. "Stop. Stop! What are you doing? No mother. No."

Caroline fell into her son's arms and dropped the pillow to the floor. Her body shook, and she sobbed. "He killed my baby. He killed my Harry. I hate him. I hate him."

Dagmar steadied herself. I'll kill him one day had been Harry's words, spoken in rage and anguish by the lake on the very night she had taken him into her arms. She cried for Harry that night and she would cry for Caroline this day.

George settled his mother into a chair and turned to his father. "Oh, my God. What have you done? The bastard is dead!"

Chapter 22

Dagmar looked around the room in astonishment. Karl was dead and Caroline had killed him.

No one spoke until Regina slammed down the book she had been pretending to read onto the table. "Does nothing come easy in this family? We'll burn in hell for this one, no doubt."

"Grandmother," George admonished, but could offer no rebuttal. He then added, "Let's all stay calm."

"Little late for calm," Regina said.

"I'm not kidding, grandmother. We'll have to call Dr. Jensen and if anything goes wrong, I'll take the blame."

Good Lord, Dagmar thought. Is there no end to this man's mission to save people from their impossible deeds? His mother sat calmly, staring in a blank haze. Regina was on her feet, ready to do battle. Dagmar couldn't believe what she was about to say.

"Let's not panic until we have to. His breathing was very shallow and there is every possibility he could have already passed before… Well, you know, before Caroline adjusted his pillow."

Regina laughed and sat back down. "Damn straight," she said. "I knew I was going to like this girl," she said to George.

George left the room to call Dr. Jensen. Regina turned to Dagmar and said, "You're one of us now."

The events of the day left Dagmar certain all manners and pleasantries had been completely abandoned. "That is yet to be determined, if you ask me. We'll all be lucky we don't go to jail. I'm not a part of all this," she said.

"Not a part of it?" Regina snarled. "You're a big part of it. Harry fought Karl for you. His own father beat him mercilessly. His mother found him and sent him to me before he went to university. Caroline bore Karl's wrath for that one. Then George married you, trying to protect you. Your brother betrayed you by trying to protect you and your family from Karl's scourge. If Karl hadn't fallen to the floor with a stroke, your husband would be going to jail for murder, protecting his family, even from itself. Where would you be then? What would you do to protect your family, Dagmar? And you are most definitely a part of this."

Regina's remarks were like a slap in the face, a jolt of lightning from hell. Dagmar balled her fists, as if ready to strike in anger. She looked Regina straight in the eye. "You're right. I'm not some lost little child anymore, and I only wish I had such courage."

The door opened and Dr. Jensen and George came in. The doctor quietly examined the body for any signs of life. He took a deep breath and looked to a broken and worn Caroline, still lost in a haze. He glanced down at the pillow resting on the floor next to her and then back to Karl.

112

"Was he alone when he passed?" the doctor asked.

Dagmar's throat was dry, and her palms were sweating. A bird chirped outside, breaking the long silence. "I came in just after dinner to sit with my father-in-law. Caroline was tired and needed to rest."

The doctor took a long, steady look at Dagmar. He raised his hand to his chin and slowly nodded his head before speaking. "You're the picture of your mother when she was young. A good, honest woman who always did what was best for her family." He turned to the bed and placed his stethoscope back in his bag. "I'm done here, and I'll send you some help. I'll leave some sedatives for Caroline so she can finally truly rest. This matter is closed."

Dagmar found herself, once again, in the same cemetery where sweet Myrtle lay. Nearly the whole town had gathered that day to comfort the Christianson family.

Today, Karl Hanson was buried. Caroline was not strong enough to attend. Regina stood next to Dagmar and her grandson. The Christianson family and a bank representative completed the circle of mourners. Such was the testimony to the wealth and accomplishments of Karl Hanson.

Sitting in the front parlor of the Hanson house, it had been just over a month since Dagmar and George had arrived back in Minaka Falls. Their belongings had been sent, and they were set to begin their new life.

Not quite certain if Dr. Jensen had believed her, or if somehow Mamma's gentle reach had protected her, Dagmar sensed it was done. Now was a time for second chances. Surely there had to be better times for them. George deserved better than this. She deserved better and vowed to make them happy. She wondered if a second chance to be a mother rested inside her. Time would tell.

Regina walked into the room and settled into the chair near Dagmar. "Caroline is mending, and I'm growing restless. It's time for me to go," she said.

Dagmar had come to admire and appreciate Regina. She was straightforward and decisive, qualities she was striving to master.

"I think a nice long voyage to Europe will do both Caroline and me some good. Karl wouldn't allow her to travel in the past and I think she needs a change from this place. George has taken over his father's position at the bank and has attempted to right any past mishandling. You and George have settled in here and need to make this place your own."

"Please don't leave on our account. We can find a house and not be in the way," Dagmar said, feeling embarrassed to have been a burden.

"Nonsense. You belong here. The deed is in my name. I didn't trust Karl when I helped them move here, so I want to make you a deal."

Dagmar was curious what she meant by making you a deal but sat quietly, waiting to see what Regina had in mind.

"I'm going to transfer the deed into your name," Regina said.

"What? Why would you do that?" Dagmar couldn't believe what she was hearing.

"There are wrongs that have been done to you and need to be righted. I'm going to have George open an account in your name. There will be enough money for you to remodel this house and make it a home for you and my grandson. Fill it with happiness and, God willing, grandchildren. A woman needs her own money and power. Caroline had money, but allowed her power to be taken." Regina sighed. "Make this the happy home it was meant to be."

Dagmar remembered Lili saying, "Don't look back, it's nothing but a bucket of tears. We're all princesses, or at least we should be." Lili was right. It was time to stop looking back. She wasn't certain about being a princess, but maybe she could build a little castle for her and George and maybe fill it with happiness.

"But don't worry, I've not forgotten about Marta. We'll hire another detective to search for her. I'm certain we'll bring her home one day.

One day, Dagmar thought. Her hopes had been dashed in the past. There was no telling where Lili had taken her, just as there was no telling what hers and George's future would bring. She thought of Papa, coming to a new life, far from his homeland. He and Mamma built their little castle, filled with joy and laughter. She wanted that, and maybe this was her chance.

"Don't stay away too long, Regina. I want you here when our baby is born."

"Baby?" Regina embraced her with tears and hugs, full of all the dreams and best wishes for the future. "We'll be home again soon, but for now take care of George and our new little one," she said, hugging Dagmar once again.

Chapter 23

1929

The stock market fell in October, and young Harold was born just after the New Year. George and Dagmar wanted to honor Harry and the loss they both had endured. He was going to need a lot of honor, courage, and determination to face what was to be endured, Dagmar thought. It had taken a few months for the effects of the crash to reach Minaka Falls, but when the morning run on the bank occurred, they knew there would be hard times ahead.

Regina and Caroline returned from Europe with grave news of both economic and political strife. "Unemployment is worse there and there is talk of new tariffs. The political talk is ugly and concerning. I'm uncertain how the world will fare," Regina said.

"Ja, this is not good," Papa insisted. "The fascists and thugs are like slithering snakes terrifying good people everywhere they go. They take what they want, lining their pockets with gold and power. I've seen it before. These will be sad times for many," Papa said, shaking his head. "We must be cautious going forward."

"We can be cautious tomorrow," Dagmar commanded. "Tonight, we celebrate little Harold and the return of family. She reached for George's hand on the table beside her but felt him trembling. She squeezed his hand to reassure him but saw a look of fear in his eye.

"Dagmar is right," Olga said. "Let's all talk about my birthday party instead."

Mamma laughed, "Yes, Olga, let's all talk about you."

The gathering had ended, and everyone headed home or settled in for the night. Dagmar placed her baby in his bassinet near their bed. She snuggled up under the covers, moving closer to her husband.

"Honey, we need to talk," George said.

"What's wrong?"

"Your father is right. These are serious times. Grandmother's quick investment saved the bank, but a lot of the farms are failing, and several businesses won't make it through summer. That fire last month didn't help either. They will not rebuild the sawmill. That means jobs will be lost and less money spent in town. He's right. Some will line their pockets, but most won't. Your father's dealership is struggling. I think he is too proud to ask for help," George said.

"What do you mean, struggling?"

George straightened the covers. "He was late on his payment to the bank this month. People aren't buying many new cars and the farmers are buying nothing. No tractors, no trucks, nothing," he sighed.

Dagmar's heart pounded. "What can we do?" She sat up, praying George had a plan.

"I think you need to ask your father for a job."

"A job? What about Harold?" Dagmar leaned back against the headboard of the big, sprawling new bed.

George said, "Yes, a job. Mother and grandmother can help with the baby. You've finished remodeling the house and I think your father needs you. His partner, Arne, has stepped aside and his son, Roland, has taken his place."

"I don't like Roland," Dagmar spouted.

"Neither do I, but nonetheless, he is maneuvering things at the dealership."

"What do you mean, maneuvering things? Papa won't stand for any funny business," Dagmar insisted.

"I know, I know, dear. I'm not sure what he's up to, but there have been a lot of rumors down at the Mason's lodge. I can't put my finger on it yet, but I know he's up to no good. I'm keeping my eye on him."

"Ok, I'll speak to Papa tomorrow. If you're sure you don't mind me not being home all day. I had intended to ask you one day when Harold was older if you thought women working out of the home was a good thing, but I thought it was too soon," Dagmar said.

George gave his wife a tender kiss. "Honey, it will be okay. Your father needs you and I'm certain my mother and grandmother will be happy to spoil young Harold even more. Times are changing and your father needs your help," he said stroking his fingers through her soft hair.

"What about you?" Dagmar said, snuggling closer in his arms.

"You always spoil me, my dear," George said. "I'm sorry I'm not as exciting and adventurous as Harry was, but I hope you…"

"Hope what?" Dagmar said. "I love you, George. The past is the past. We can't change that. Lars once said that I bury my head in the past and don't see those in front of me. I think a lot about Lars these days, and think he was right. Sometimes the past begins to look different from what it really was. We remember what we want to remember and perhaps it wasn't as we thought. I'm not that lost, desperate child you once saved. I'm here because I want to be, and I know you are the love I was meant to have. Now hush, while we have the time to spoil each other," she said before she turned back and shut the side table light out.

Dagmar started to work two days later. Everyone was excited for her, except Olga.

"When I asked Papa for a job, he said no," Olga complained.

"He doesn't need any more people to sell cars. He would have to let someone else go to hire you." Dagmar never ceased to be amazed at Olga's juvenile logic. "If you want to help me with the books, I'll speak to him."

"And sit back in that dusty old room with you? I don't think so. My complexion needs sun and air. Oh my gosh, here comes Roland! How do I look? Is he staring at me? He is just so handsome." Olga turned and smiled, "Hello Roland, I didn't know you were working today." She fluttered her eyelashes.

"I work every day, gorgeous. I was just about to go to lunch."

Dagmar didn't care for how Roland was eyeing her little sister up and down. Even more, she didn't care for how Olga seemed to wallow in the attention. She made a mental note to have a little heart-to-heart with her when they were alone next.

Papa walked up to the desk. "Dagmar, here are the parts invoices for the year so far and all the shipping invoices I can find," he said.

"This is what I'm talking about, Papa. You can't balance your income and expenses without a proper system," she said.

"It's all right, dear. Set up any system you think will help. Roland can help you. He knows what parts come and go. I'm heading home to check on Mamma quickly. I'll be back in an hour."

When Papa had set the parts invoices on the table, Dagmar thought she saw Roland tense, but when she looked back up from the pile of papers, Roland and Olga were strolling out the door.

Papa returned promptly in one hour, and Dagmar felt the need to speak to him. "Papa, may I have a word?"

"Certainly," he said, sitting down in the extra chair next to her table. "Looks like you've been hard at work."

"I have, Papa, and things are not adding up. You have more shipping invoices for parts received than you have receipts. So, either the inventory is wrong or there are missing parts. We need to address this immediately," Dagmar said in a serious tone.

"This is not good," Papa said.

"No. Not good at all. I think it is best if I go back and check all entries for the past year or so. We need to do a new inventory and compare it to what is listed. This is likely to take us a couple of weeks, but I'm worried." Dagmar shuffled the papers together in one neat stack. "You do realize this is serious, don't you, Papa?"

Papa frowned but rose to get up. "Hopefully it's just a mix up," he said, walking away.

Dagmar sat in the front parlor after dinner that night, completely exhausted. Caroline and Regina went to bed early after a full day with young Harold. She kept reviewing, over and over, some of the figures in her head.

"You look intense, my dear," George said.

"I'm sorry," Dagmar said, looking to her husband. "I think you are right. The dealership is in trouble. I've just started, but the books aren't adding up. Invoices are missing everywhere. I'm not sure what's going on, but I'm worried."

"Any clues at all?" George asked.

"Not yet, but a strange thing happened when Papa brought me some of the ledgers and invoices. Roland had been flirting like a rogue with Olga."

George laughed. "So, flirting with your baby sister is the problem?"

"No, but I don't like that either," she said before pausing. "Roland saw the stack of invoices and looked a little panicked."

"You think he is stealing?"

"I don't know. It will take us a couple of weeks to sort things out, but this doesn't look good. There's a lot of unaccountable inventory that's gone somewhere. I'm pretty sure Roland knows exactly where that somewhere is.

"I wouldn't be surprised. He's not got the best reputation in town. I want you to be careful around him and I think you should speak to Olga as well," George said.

"I think you're correct, but I think I'm exhausted. Tomorrow will be soon enough to sort this out."

George pulled his wife up out of her chair and into his arms. "I think it's time I take my two favorite babies to bed." He pulled her tighter for one more kiss.

The phone rang on the table in the front foyer by the bottom of the stairs. George stole another quick kiss on her forehead and left the room to answer the call.

Dagmar gathered up young Harold, who had been sleeping peacefully on the sofa next to his father. The moment George walked back into the room, she knew something was wrong. "Please don't let it be Mamma," she whispered to herself.

"There's a fire at the dealership. I want you to stay here, but I'm going to see if I can help. Get some rest. Tomorrow may be a difficult day."

"Rest. I can't rest. I'm coming with you. Your mother and Regina can take care of Harold. This is my family and my Papa's livelihood," Dagmar said.

"All right then, but remember this is our family, not just yours, and we'll be there together," George insisted. "How bad can it be?"

Chapter 24

Dagmar arrived the next morning, and the office was an utter shamble. The walls were blackened; the furniture burned, and every single file had been destroyed. The volunteer fire department ruled a cigarette had been left burning near a pile of papers on the worktable. Dagmar was livid. She was primarily the only person in the office and had never smoked a cigarette in her life.

"This will take us weeks to set up a new system, but we're going to do it right this time. Every receipt and nickel will be accounted for," she said looking directly at Roland. "We're purchasing a fireproof safe and only Papa will have the combination. This is for everyone's protection, but primarily for the protection of the company. A new inventory will be taken, and I'll hire an outside staff to complete the task. We'll talk to George to see if the bank can give us some time on our next payment, but they want to see progress. We have no choice," she said hoping they understood the seriousness of the problem.

Roland laughed. "Well, little missy, let me know when you get the place cleaned up. I'm going to lunch," he said.

Papa did his best to calm Dagmar. "I'll get a few people in here and get this straightened out. We'll get a fresh coat of paint and some new furniture. You'll see, it will be fine."

"Fine," Dagmar repeated. "The man is an idiot, a complete disaster."

"It will be fine," Papa said walking out the door, throwing his hands into the air.

"Who's an idiot?" Olga said strolling into the office.

"Roland! He's the most condescending, arrogant fool I've ever met, and I don't want you to see him again!" Dagmar shouted.

"You don't have any right to tell me what to do. I'm nineteen and old enough to see whoever I want to," Olga stated.

"You're my sister, and I don't like him." Dagmar was befuddled how Olga couldn't see the man was simply no good.

"You're not my sister. You're Myrtle's sister. Ever since your precious twin died you pushed the rest of us away. Even when Myrtle was alive, I wasn't good enough for you two. Lars calls and writes to you all the time, and you just ignore him," Olga said.

"What are you talking about?" Dagmar felt her knees weakening. "Lars betrayed me and…"

"That's a lie! Poor, poor Dagmar. Everybody feels sorry for Dagmar!" Olga shouted now. "Lars tried to protect you, not just from Karl. You don't like Roland? Well, your judgement with Harry wasn't so great either, was it? You've got a rich husband, although I don't know why he puts up with you. You spend more time in the past than with those in front of you. I'll do as I damn well please and you, Miss high-and-mighty

Dagmar with the fancy car and house, can go to hell."

The door slammed behind Olga, before Dagmar had a chance to respond. Tears welled in her eyes, and she thought her heart would burst. She knew how Harry felt that day by the lake when she hurled nasty judgements upon him. What did stupid, spoiled Olga know anyway? she thought.

Papa opened the door and handed Dagmar her purse. "Go home, my darling. Things will sort themselves. You've done enough today," he said putting his arm around her shoulder and guiding her out. "Families sometimes fuss with one another. I'll speak to your sister. Now, go home and enjoy the day with my grandson. We'll get this cleaned up. Tomorrow will be better," Papa said leading her forward.

Dagmar had walked the eight blocks home. With each step, Olga's words pounded in her head. She was tempted as she walked past the church to stop by and chat with Myrtle but resisted, not wanting to give credence to her sister's nastiness.

Once inside her house, Dagmar plopped down on the sofa in a heap of exhaustion and wounded pride. Young Harold was sprawled out on a blanket on the floor and Regina was in pursuit of a much-needed cup of strong coffee. She watched him wiggle about pushing and turning to make his way about. He looked up giving her a radiant smile, followed by an endless gurgling, and babbling of baby magic. She inched down onto the floor and took him into her arms.

"You're growing so fast, my little man," she said, hugging him closer. Her thought immediately went to Marta. "You have a sister, Harold. She doesn't live with us because someone else is taking care of her far away."

Dagmar prayed it was true. She is six now and I think she would be a very nice sister to you, she thought.

"Oh gosh," she said putting her son back on the blanket. "I hate your nasty Auntie Olga," she quipped before Regina came into the room.

"What's this. You and your sister are locking horns again?"

Dagmar wasn't sure how the conversation had gotten so out of control, but she was certain Olga was wrong. "She said I live in the past and ignore everyone in front of me. Then she called me Miss high-and-mighty and said she didn't know why George put up with me. She's such a spoiled brat. I don't know why I put up with *her*," Dagmar huffed.

Regina chuckled. "Oh my, that does sound like a ruckus, but that's what families are for. What made her get into such a tizzy in the first place?"

"Hmm, I suppose it was my fault. She's smitten with that horrible man, Roland. I basically told her not to see him, and that really didn't go well." She paused, biting her lower lip.

"And" Regina said.

"And I guess she may be right. She's not a child anymore, but I just don't like him. He's arrogant and always seems to be sneaking around up to no good. I can't put my finger on it, but I'm pretty certain he is why the books were off, and then the fire," Dagmar said.

"Do you have proof?"

"No, but…."

"The answer is no. You'll just have to keep an eye out, and you've warned your sister. It is her choice now. The heart makes fools of us from time to time. My daughter is proof of that. Olga will be fine." Regina laid her hand on Dagmar's knee. "Perhaps you should give some thought to her other observations."

Regina's hand was soft and gentle, but her words cut straight

126

through Dagmar. "You agree with her? You think I live in the past and I'm not a good wife to George?"

"Not what I said. You've been through a lot. Not knowing where dear Marta is, is a terrible burden, but you have a fine young son and a husband who adores you. Perhaps it time to look ahead and allow yourself to be happy." Regina patted her hand on her knee then turned to pour the coffee.

No more was said for the remainder of the day. Dagmar pondered the words of wisdom and anger each woman had said to her. She knew Olga loved her and she loved her sister, but they needed to talk, and she needed to support her sister. She had all but said the same words to George the night before. Maybe she was still a bit of a lost child, and perhaps it was time she gave Lars a ring. She really had missed him.

Next, she would plan a picnic. How she had loved picnics by the lake when she was little, and George and young Harold would have the same. She smiled, satisfied with her new resolve, but was absolutely, totally certain, she was not ever forgetting Myrtle or Marta and would never ever like Roland, ever.

Chapter 25

It had been two weeks since Dagmar had last seen Olga. It was just like her lovely, little spoiled brat sister to make her suffer, but this was ridiculous, she thought. Every time she had stopped by Mamma and Papa's house, Olga was out. It took little to figure out who she was with, but she had vowed to support her sister, and let the impending disaster of Roland run its course.

Dagmar stretched back in her office chair and yawned. The day had been busy, but the new system was finally in place and a strict inventory of the entire dealership had been completed the day before. She looked out the tiny window Papa had insisted be installed for her during the renovations.

"You need a little sunshine in here," he had said.

Her heart pounded as her worst nightmare was about to unfold. Roland was huddled in the back corner of the lot, where she was certain he thought no one could see what he was up to. Leaning against a truck was none other than her evil, bastard cousin Marvin. The two were fussing back and forth, shaking their fists, and shouting at one another. Marvin pushed Roland. Roland defiantly stood his ground until suddenly it all seemed to be resolved. Roland pulled out a large roll of money and handed it to Marvin. Each shook hands and Marvin climbed into his truck and drove on away.

All the memories of that miserable winter, locked away in a tiny shed with Lili came rushing back. They had narrowly escaped with their lives, but Dagmar cringed remembering how ruthlessly Marvin had beaten and raped Lili. Then he followed her to Duluth. Thank God, George had saved her. A shiver ran up her neck. What was he doing here in Minaka Falls and why did Roland give him money? A lot of money, she thought.

Roland would most likely make himself scarce for the rest of the day, but Dagmar knew this could not wait. Whatever he was up to, she was going to find out. She thought and thought. Where did Roland get that kind of money? Most people were cash poor and there were few signs of the Depression letting up. He was known to gamble, but no one in town had that kind of money and why would he give it to Marvin, she wondered. Things just didn't add up. She would have to discuss this with Papa.

Coming out of her office, she ran a collision course straight into Roland. She bumped up against him, almost face to face. The overwhelming stench of whiskey permeated everywhere. Dagmar held her breath and stepped back into the office.

"What the hell?" Roland said, giving Dagmar a stern look.

"I saw you out back. I know you're up to something that involves Marvin and I want to know what it is," she demanded.

"That's none of your business."

"Well, we'll just have to let Papa decide whose business it is."

Roland pushed her further back into the office and shut the door behind him. "Don't threaten me. I'm not scared of you like your little whiny sister is. I can take care of myself," he said.

Dagmar felt nauseous. His breath sickened her. "You bastard. You're running whiskey, aren't you?" She stood her ground, but there was no mistaking the shift in his demeanor. His eyes turned dark and intense with anger, and she took a step back. "Don't bother to lie. Marvin and his buddies have stills. Whiskey's illegal under prohibition, not to mention you're crossing state lines involving that low life."

"You don't know what you're talking about, and how do you know about Marvin?" Roland laughed.

Dagmar shifted her stance. No one needed to know about her and Marvin. "He's my cousin, and everyone knows his father and brothers chased him out of town. If you're running whiskey, you'll ruin Papa's reputation and get arrested," Dagmar said, feeling more vulnerable every second.

Roland took a step back and then slowly started to inch his way around her. Eyeing her up and down, before he spoke, "Ruin Papa's reputation? I think you've already done that. Tell me about your secret, Dagmar. What's your little lie? Marvin told me all about you and your little whoring half-breed friend. Does George know? How about your Mamma, Papa, your sister, brother, and that rich grandmother of George's. Does she know?"

Dagmar felt the room closing in on her. George and Regina were not a problem, but others were. It would break Papa's heart. Lars already knew, and she supposed Olga would find out eventually, but there was young Harold to consider. A scandal like this could ruin not only Papa, but her entire family and her son's future. She couldn't let that happen.

"Cat got your tongue? I think it's time you and I go on about our business and stay out of each other's way. I'll keep your secret. You keep mine and we'll be just one big happy family," he said and then gave an evil, sarcastic laugh.

Dagmar knew she had no choice but to let it go. He had trapped her, and, unlike him, she wasn't willing to destroy everyone she loved. She took a deep breath and said, "We'll both forget about Marvin, but no more stolen parts. I can't hide that, and I don't want any of it here at the dealership."

"No problem, sister girl. We hide it up on the reservation. It's foolproof, feds can't go anywhere near it. Then we haul it on up to Fargo to a big buyer. If I play my cards right, I'll be out of your hair before you know it, and you can stay Daddy's perfect little girl. Just don't cross me again," he said before walking away.

The door shut, and Dagmar sat back down at her desk. The bastard had her, at least for now. He called her 'sister girl' and said they were one big happy family. Roland was no brother and was certainly no part of her family. The damn arrogant fool didn't even feel the need to hide the details of his operation. He even bragged about it. Papa always said, "Pride goeth before the fall," and Roland was going to fall. She just had to figure out how that was going to happen. She needed to talk to George. There would be no more secrets between them, and it was going to take more than her to get rid of Roland.

Chapter 26

Dagmar rushed home, full of concern. Olga would have to wait. First she would need to see what George thought about the whole Roland mess. She set her belongings down on the catch all bench as she came in the door.

"We're in here, in the dining room!" George shouted. "I've got a surprise for you."

Oh great, Dagmar thought. Just what I need is another surprise today. She was exhausted and in no mood for excessive chatter and merriment. She could smell Regina's famous roasted chicken and garlic potatoes, which was at least a promising sign.

"Lars!" she squealed as she entered the room. "I didn't know you were coming to town."

"Like George said, it's a surprise and here's another surprise. I want you to meet my wife, Ellen," Lars said beaming with pride.

"Married? My goodness, Ellen, let me hug you. When did all

this happen?" Dagmar was too preoccupied with delight for her brother to notice Roland and Olga sitting at the far end of the dining room table.

"We thought we would surprise everyone over the holidays, but things have changed. Ellen is expecting a baby, and we're moving back to Minaka Falls," Lars said.

"A baby. You're coming home. Oh my gosh, did you tell Mamma yet? I can't believe this," Dagmar said embracing her brother, when suddenly she looked, and her eyes met Roland's. What the hell was he doing here? She felt her fists balling in anger. So much for staying out of each other's way, she thought.

Roland smirked and gave a little wave. He took Olga's hand in his and it was then that Dagmar glimpsed the ring on Olga's finger. She fought the urge to march straight into the kitchen and retrieve the meat cleaver. This was completely unacceptable.

"I tried to get Mamma and Papa to come, but they said it had been too exciting a day for them and they needed to rest," Lars said. "Papa looked exhausted, and Mamma looked pale. Is everything ok?"

Dagmar sat in the chair next to her husband and looked straight at Olga. "These are exhausting days. The dealership had a fire and we're working hard to put things back in place. These are difficult times, and some people make it even more difficult." The tone in her voice was rising, and so was her urge to throttle her baby sister.

Olga stared back at her older sister with a smug defiance. She smiled and asked, "So, Lars, are you going to set up a practice here in Minaka Falls?"

"I'm joining Dr. Jensen. He's getting on in years, but don't tell him I said that." He laughed with everyone else. "The town is growing, and this Depression can't last forever. There will be new families needing medical care and I want my children to grow up with family. Life in the city is hectic and unpredictable."

"There certainly is a lot of unpredictability around here, it seems," Dagmar said slamming her fork down on the table. The dishes rattled and everyone looked from Dagmar to Olga.

Olga continued to munch on her vegetables and ignored all the eyes staring at her, especially those of her sister.

"Dagmar," George said with concern.

"Don't 'Dagmar' me," Dagmar said screeching her chair back and standing oblivious to the shock of those around her. "That better not be a ring on your finger, Olga Marie Christianson."

The room was silent. Olga looked first at her sister and then to her brother and his wife. "I'm so glad you are moving back home. Now maybe our dear sister can worry about someone else's life or maybe just mind her own business. Yes, I'm married, and Roland is my husband. That's why Mamma and Papa were frazzled and that's why we're leaving." Olga stood, pushed back her chair, then she and Roland left the table and walked out the door.

"Welcome home," Lars said to everyone with a toast of his glass. "I take it this was unexpected?"

Dagmar finally sat back down. "It's not only unexpected. It's a disaster. She's too young and Roland…" she grumbled. "He's…"

"He's what?" Lars said. "He's her choice, and she is old enough. We're going to have to accept this as a family and welcome him, just as I hope you will welcome Ellen."

Dagmar sighed, tapped her foot ferociously beneath the table and knew it was time to surrender, at least for tonight. Roland hadn't said a word but had set her up and played her for a fool in front of her family. "I'm sorry. It was just a shock. I'll speak to her tomorrow."

Dinner had ended not long after Olga left. Lars and Ellen said their goodbyes and promised to see them again soon. Dagmar went upstairs to settle young Harold into his bed for the night. She kissed him on the forehead and ran her fingers through his little curls. Please never make Mamma crazy like Auntie Olga does, she silently pleaded to her son. Marry a nice, Norwegian girl. Somebody who will make you happy and treat her kindly like your father does to me. She watched his soft little breaths move his chest, and he wiggled and stretched before settling in for a peaceful sleep. His innocence brought her such calmness, and she realized how fortunate she was to have married George.

"Coming to bed? I've been missing you," George said from the doorway.

Dagmar smiled and went to her husband's waiting arms. They embraced and kissed with long slow affection. "I'm sorry for tonight," she said as they walked into their bedroom and closed the door.

"It was an interesting night," George said pulling back the covers on the bed. "You need to rest and let your family worry about themselves. Olga is married now, whether you like it or not. Maybe Roland isn't as bad as you think."

Gone was the calm. "As bad as I think?" Dagmar launched into a review of the entire day, from Marvin's arrival to Olga's frightening marriage. "It is as bad as I think," she said.

George was furious. "Threatened you? He threatened you?"

"I was fine. Really, George. Olga's the one in danger here," she said.

"But he threatened you, my wife. I'm not standing for that." George got up to dress. "I'm going to go take care of this right now."

Dagmar laughed.

"It's not funny," George said, now scowling at her.

"No, you're right. It's not funny," Dagmar said climbing into bed and patting it for him to return to her. "I was angry and played right into Roland's hands tonight. This is going to take more than you beating him up to solve this problem. He is arrogant, which causes you to dislike him, but I think he is just a charming, cleaner version of my cousin Marvin. I'm worried my sister is in real danger and doesn't even see it coming. He's smart and thinks all the illegal money he is making from running his whiskey will protect him, but you can only hurt and cheat so many people before someone puts a stop to it. I just don't want Olga to be hurt."

"Your family is our family, and I will not let that man hurt you or them. I promise, I'll take care of Roland.

Chapter 27

R oland and Olga left immediately for an extended honeymoon.

Lars and Ellen bought a cute Craftsman-style home on Main Street, only a short walk from his office. Mamma was feeling better, and Papa was excited the New Deal by President Roosevelt had finally brought some promise to Minaka Falls.

The government was purchasing a fleet of trucks from the dealership to aid in the new reforestation project, which meant to put some people back to work in the area. This would put the dealership back in good standing and turn a profit once again. Life settled back down into an everyday rhythm.

"Dagmar," Papa said. "Arne, my partner, is coming in next week for a couple of days. Roland should be back soon, and I need to be certain he behaves himself. Arne will keep an eye on things while I'm gone," Papa said. He shuffled a few papers on his desk trying to bring order to the day.

"Where are you going? Is Mamma okay?" Dagmar said looking anxious.

"Mamma is fine. I'm running out to the mine, out near Grizzly Lake. It may take me a few days to assess the situation. My papa was in partnership with his brother many years ago in a mining adventure, Two Brothers' Mining, on the other side of the lakes and a little north. My papa wanted a family and a farm, but my uncle dreamed of getting rich digging gold. They both put up money and started a mine. Uncle Ervin found his gold, but it was not the huge riches he had hoped for. Later he found iron ore. Mining is a dirty business full of hard work and has had a twisted history of victories and defeats. Uncle Ervin's son had maintained the mine, but it's not in good shape and my cousin died a few months ago. The whole mess has been left to me. I'm uncertain of the exact condition of the mine or the surrounding area. It doesn't produce a lot of ore right now, but I'm certain there's promise in the future," he said.

Dagmar was intrigued. "You own a mine? What do you mean, promise? If it's not producing a lot, I would think you might just sell it," she said.

Papa smiled. "Nothing much is selling during these times, unless you are willing to pretty close to give it away. My brother was certain it would be valuable one day. Some things take time to come into their own. Uncle Ervin knew that. He and his son just didn't have enough time. Maybe it's time now. One day there are going to be millions and millions of people in this country and even around the world. When times get better, which they will, everyone will want a new car. They're going to need the materials to make those cars. I just wanted to be certain you and Roland don't have any problems while I'm away."

"Don't blame me for Roland, but, if you don't mind, I'd rather go with you. If you let me," Dagmar asked.

"I would like that. This is work, but it's a pleasant drive out there. You can keep me company and I'd like a young person's input," Papa said crossing his arms looking pleased with her interest.

"Great, just let me know which day and I'll pack us a pleasant lunch. Would you mind if George came along as well?"

Papa chuckled, "George is always welcome, but Mamma will pack the lunch. You and George have a good head for business, but Mamma is the best cook."

Dagmar was delighted to be joining her father but couldn't wait to find out more information. Her first stop would be to the public library. If she hurried and skipped lunch, she just may have enough time to get what she needed.

Dagmar left the library, planning on stopping by her house and dropping off all the books on mining she had found. It wasn't a far walk. If she cut across the town square, she would be home even quicker, but then she saw Olga.

Sitting on a bench all alone, Olga looked distressed. Dagmar and her sister's relationship had been strained since Olga married Roland. She chuckled to herself, who was she kidding, it had always been strained, but it was getting better. She looked at her sister, who was unaware she was there. There was a sadness that alarmed Dagmar. Her face was pale, and it appeared she had been crying for some time.

"Olga," she said.

Olga immediately turned away trying to hide her tears.

Dagmar asked, "What's wrong?"

Her sister said nothing.

"Please Olga," Dagmar said sitting down next to her sister. "I didn't know you were back in town. Roland hasn't been to the dealership yet. Really, I want to help. I know I haven't always been the best sister, but you can tell me what's wrong."

Olga fell into Dagmar's lap sobbing tears like she had never seen.

"Please, tell me. What's wrong. I promise I won't yell at you or boss you around. Just tell me," Dagmar pleaded.

"I think I might be pregnant and I'm not sure Roland is going to be happy," she said as more tears and sobs followed.

Dagmar was at a loss what to say. She had promised not to yell at her or boss her around, but right now she just didn't know what to say, so she held her sister and rocked her all alone in the park.

"I shouldn't have married him," Olga said. "He can be kind and generous but there are times he scares me."

"Has he hurt you, Olga?" Dagmar demanded.

"No. No. It's just…. Never mind, you wouldn't understand." She sobbed again.

"Try me," Dagmar insisted.

"He's always trying to make things better for us. Roland does things he thinks are a good idea to make money for the future, but no matter how much he has it's never enough. He takes chances and does things he shouldn't. I am worried that I am not enough because he is a hard man to please."

"Olga, a good friend of mine once told me, we're all princesses, or at least we ought to be. She taught me not to let other people make me feel less about myself or tell me I'm not good enough. If Roland doesn't make you feel good

140

about yourself, then maybe…"

"Don't say that, Dagmar. It will be all right. I know I can make him happy. He's just under a lot of stress. His father is really hard on him, and you know I'm not easy. I've got to go, but please, say nothing to Papa. He doesn't like Roland, either. I've got to go." Olga rushed off before Dagmar could say anymore.

Dagmar looked at her watch. She was already twenty minutes late and would have to hurry. A little prayer for Olga and a quick-step walk to her house would have to do. Papa wouldn't take her seriously if she couldn't even be on time.

George and Dagmar were ready to go the following Wednesday. She was feeling very adventurous and ready to take on the world. Armed with all the information she had painstakingly gathered from the library, and feeling relieved Olga had called to say hers was a false alarm, the day held great promise.

"I'll drive," George announced, first thing.

Dagmar chuckled. "You shouldn't have taught me to drive if you don't enjoy being a passenger."

"I don't think your father is ready for the new, faster, modern Dagmar. Let's just take the day one step at a time."

Dagmar respected George's steadiness and calm judgement. Papa would appreciate that as well. They picked Papa up and headed out to the mine, not much over twenty minutes away. It was a worn-down building manned by a foreman and a few young secretaries, each performing a specific task. There was a young boy named Jimmy, not more than ten or so, sweeping up and running errands. Dagmar wondered why he wasn't in school. His clothes were worn, and he wasn't even wearing shoes.

"Come, Dagmar, we have more to see," George urged, looking intense. "I think your father is about done touring this disaster and is ready to leave. There's a lot of work to be done around here." He sighed.

Dagmar's heart sank. She had really been excited to take on a new challenge and, even looking around, there were possibilities, as Papa would say.

"What do you think?" Papa said waiting patiently for their opinions.

George was first to speak. "Hans," he said, speaking like a banker. "It is going to take some investment to bring this place back up to speed. It could be done slowly, but you're talking a lot of work and a hefty investment. It'll take a strong commitment and a lot of long hours. Workers won't be a problem. Lord knows there's plenty of good men out of work, but you'll have to put a good team together. It could be difficult, at best."

"What do you think, Dagmar?" Papa asked.

Dagmar looked first at Papa and then to George. They were treating her as an equal and she felt the weight of that enormous trust. A swift wind blew from the north and dust filled the air. She coughed and waved her hand in front of her face to clear the dust away. Looking up, she saw young Jimmy standing on the porch of the slightly dilapidated old building and knew her heart.

"I think the mine is just like that young man over there. Neglected and forgotten, but with a little love and effort, could be something quite special," she said.

Chapter 27

"Ja," Papa said in joyous agreement, and it was agreed, they were in the mining business.

Chapter 28

D agmar stopped by with a few essentials she thought might help the newlyweds. She was surprised to see how quickly Lars and Ellen had transformed their little Craftsman house into a home. There was a cozy, welcoming feeling as soon as she stepped on the wide-open front porch with plants already placed between the short fat columns and a swing begging to be sat upon hung from the broad rafters.

This was a home where love would grow, Dagmar thought.

"Morning," Ellen said as she opened the stained-glass door. "I saw you coming up the walk. Please come in."

"I've brought you a few small things, and Mamma has sent some of her best doilies and pillowcases." She stepped inside, looked around the room, and said, "This is just lovely, Ellen."

"Thank you so much. Let's sit. I've just made some tea and there may be some rolls left if your brother hasn't eaten them all." She laughed.

"I remember. When we were children, Papa said we had one

garden to feed the family and one to feed Lars," she said and joined in the laughter.

The women moved to the small table in the kitchen. Ellen was obviously older than Lars, and Dagmar thought she appeared to be the touch of strength and steadiness that complimented her brother.

"Have you known my brother long?" she asked.

Ellen's smile was warm and loving. "He and my husband were colleagues. They studied together and were quite good friends."

"Husband?" Dagmar was shocked. Her brother's life had been a distant memory for her since Harry's disappearance and Karl's death. She hadn't really blamed Lars for the lost life she and Harry could have had, or that Marta had been lost in all the chaos, but she had allowed it to fester like an untreated wound.

"Lars and David were in school together and did their final training at the same hospital. Not quite two years ago, I was at work at the same hospital. I'm a pediatric nurse and was doing the night shift in the children's wing. A fire broke out in our home. David managed to pull our young son out, but both he and my Andrew had inhaled too much smoke. Neither survived the night. It nearly killed me, as well," she said.

"I'm so sorry, Ellen." Dagmar said, reaching for her hand and seeing the raw pain in her tear-filled eyes. "I can't imagine how you feel."

Ellen's hands trembled. "My parents are both gone, and David and Andrew were my only family. I drifted into a dark depression, but Lars refused to give up on me. He talked about you a lot in those days. He said you had been lost in the same darkness after your twin sister died."

Dagmar felt the sting of those memories and sensed an immediate sisterhood to Ellen. Each had known enormous loss for a loved one, and each had known the loss of a child. She prayed Marta was well, but the absence was just as real.

"Your brother misses you and your family. He worries about your mother and your sister. Most of all he worries you will never forgive him," Ellen said.

"Lars is my brother. He must know I love him," Dagmar's voice was strained.

"You might have to remind him. But remember, love and forgiveness are two different things. I had to forgive myself for not being home to protect my family when they perished that horrible night. Lars has not forgiven himself for not protecting his family, either."

Goodbyes were said as Dagmar left her welcoming gifts behind, but she carried away a new gift, the possibility to heal one loss. Lars was her only brother, and she had missed him.

Plans for the mine were coming together. Everyone was certain this Depression couldn't last forever. Small things were improving slowly. The New Deal was putting some people back to work, but it wasn't enough to bring things even close to right. There wasn't a lot of money for new cars. Even those who weren't hungry worried they could be next.

The dealership had improved business in parts to repair everyone's cars since the new inventory system had been put in place. Roland's secret whiskey running kept him away from the dealership and out of Dagmar's hair, for which she was thankful.

Every day was full, a nonstop hustle and bustle. Today Dagmar would head back out to the mine to see how things were coming along there. Regina had offered to invest in the mine on behalf of her grandchildren, of which she continued to hope for more.

"Olga," Dagmar said with surprise. "Is everything all right?"

"Yes, but I'm feeling a little restless and wanted to see if you could have lunch with me."

Dagmar took a deep breath but saw the pleading in her sister's eyes. Roland, however unscrupulous, had proven to be a good provider to Olga. She had a new hat, coat, or outfit every other week and a nice spending allowance, but what she didn't have was his time and attention. Olga was lonely.

"Please," Olga begged.

"I'm sorry. I just can't. I'm on my way to pick little Harold up. I'm taking him on the drive out to mine. I've been so busy I feel like I don't spend enough time with him, so off we go on a little adventure," she chuckled.

Olga's eyes lit up. "Can I go, too?"

"That would be great. You can help me keep an eye on him. He likes to run and chatters on about everything. I don't know how Caroline and Regina keep up with him all day," she laughed.

The journey out to the mine seemed like nothing as Harold talked endlessly about maybe getting a puppy for his birthday or possibly a hot-air balloon.

"A hot-air balloon." Dagmar laughed.

"Yup, Dad told me all about them. You go way up high and can travel all over the world. You could even take me to school every day, when I start next year, but I think I really want a puppy instead. Okay?"

Olga and Dagmar laughed and laughed at Harold's determined innocence before they pulled up to the old mine office. The young orphan boy, Jimmy ran from the door to meet them.

"Morning, Jimmy," Dagmar said.

"Morning, ma'am," Jimmy said, eagerly awaiting his now traditional gift.

"I have a surprise for you." Dagmar opened the car door and young Harold jumped out. Jimmy looked confused and a bit disappointed. Dagmar laughed and then said, "This is my son, Harold. He's come to spend the afternoon with you, and I've brought us all a picnic lunch."

"A picnic." Jimmy's eyes sparkled. "What's a picnic?"

Dagmar had become quite fond of the young boy on her many trips out to the mine. She knew little about him, other than he was an orphan and seemed to make do on his own as so many children of the Depression were forced to do. "It's a basket with all sorts of goodies for the four of us. This is my sister, Olga," she said.

"She's pretty, like you," Jimmy replied. "When can we eat?"

"Why don't you help Olga with the basket? I'll go deliver my papers and join you soon. Don't eat everything before I get back." She chuckled but was certain he hadn't had a real meal in some time.

"No problem. I'm a great help. Come on, Harold, I'll show you my rock collection after we eat. I think one of them is real gold. I might be rich." Jimmy took the younger boy's hand as they walked away to the nearby table and bench.

Dagmar finished up quickly and enjoyed the merriment of the boys running about. She couldn't help but notice Jimmy's general condition. She made a mental note to bring him some shoes and possibly a new pair of pants and a shirt, she supposed.

"Do you remember when we used to run like that and laugh about nothing? We didn't have a care in the world," Olga said.

"That was before Myrtle died," Dagmar whispered as they each paused. "Those were hard times, after."

"Do the hard times ever end?" Olga looked off in the distance.

Dagmar was worried about her younger sister. She had a way of riling her at every turn, but this she did not like. "I think we need to head home and I think we need to talk to Papa about giving you a job."

"A job. Roland won't like that. A job," she said again. "What would I do?"

"Just what you did today. Help me run things back and forth to the mine and help us coordinate our new plans. Just do it part time to start so you don't interfere in Roland's time. He's out of town a lot and can't blame you for wanting to keep busy."

"Okay. I'll think about it, but I think yes." Olga hugged her sister.

"Good. We're settled. It's getting late, so let's drop Jimmy down at the mine village and head on home," Dagmar said.

They loaded the boys up in the car and headed on their way to the village driving down a bumpy, rutted road. It was shocking. The houses were nothing like those in town. They were little more than tar paper shacks, each with a small garden and scraggily clothesline. Dagmar looked over at Olga and then slowly inched on.

"Right there!" Jimmy shouted. "That's my shed."

Dagmar was mortified. Flashes of her and Lili in their small, dingy shed came rushing back. This was even smaller. She had never imagined things were like this for the miners, let alone for Jimmy. "I thought you lived with a family," she said.

"Nope. It's just me. I can take care of myself," he said with pride.

Dagmar smiled. This one has Lili's determination, she thought. Her mind was made up. This had to change. She would speak to Papa and George, but in the meantime, there was Jimmy. She stopped the car, but before he could climb out, she spoke. "I need a favor from you," she said.

"Sure. I can help."

"I need you to come to my house and help me out with Harold. He needs someone to teach him how to run and play and do things boys do. Can you help me?" Dagmar knew he was just like her Lili and thought himself capable of conquering the world, no matter how desperate his circumstances were. He was a fierce, but slightly haggard little prince, as all young boys should be, she thought to herself.

"Do I get paid?" Jimmy asked.

"We'll see what we can do," Dagmar said, laughing.

Olga looked to her sister and said, "Sure are handing out lots of jobs to those in need today, aren't you?"

"Like Papa always says, we gotta stick together. We're family. I guess mine just grew."

The ride home was quiet, as Harold slept on Jimmy's lap and Dagmar and Olga basked in the joy of being sisters.

Chapter 29

Spring 1932

A crash of noise came from George's study, followed by hushed conversation. "What are you boys up to in there?" George called, uncertain if he really wanted to know. When he walked in the room, the two boys were entangled and sprawled on the floor. Jimmy was laughing and Harold was sitting on top of him.

"That's how you wrestle a giant!" Harold shouted victoriously.

"That's not fair, little brother, if you tickle the giant he will eat you," Jimmy said as he rolled his brother off and pretended to eat him, Harold screaming in delight.

George smiled. He was elated to be the father of two young boys.

"Perhaps you two giants should go play outside," Dagmar said as she walked into the room wrapping her arms around her husband.

"Come on," Harold commanded his brother. "Let's go climb

our big tree. You can build us a fort again, but I'm the captain this time."

Off they ran as Dagmar shouted, "Not too high now. I want no broken bones. Your Uncle Lars is tired of patching you two up." She laughed and motioned for her husband to sit down and enjoy the momentary quiet.

"Those two," George said.

"I know. If only we had their energy, we could conquer the world," Dagmar laughed.

"Not if I tickle the giant, you won't." He leaned in pretending to tickle her. "Then I shall ravish you with kisses if that doesn't work," he said, kissing her in a wild pretense.

"I surrender. I surrender," Dagmar moaned and kissed her husband. "But it is the middle of the day, and you are due at an early Mason's meeting," she said.

"I'm wounded," George teased. "I really don't want to go to this meeting. Can't I just stay here and build you a fort?" he said, attempting to tease and nibble on her neck once again.

"No. No fort. You've already built us a fine home, and my sister is coming over soon. Why do you not want to go to the lodge?" she asked.

George grumbled. "I love my wonderful family, except for one family member."

"Roland," they both said in unison.

"He's become the never-ending talk of the town. His flashy car, rolls of money, and endless arrogance are beginning to annoy certain people. He's been banned from the Mason's Hall and there has been talk of putting an end to his illegal enterprises. I'm worried where this may go next," he sighed.

"We can only hope they run him out of town," Dagmar said. "But I worry about my sister."

152

"Olga will be fine," George assured her. "Your father and I will make certain of that. I suppose I should get going. Your father will need Lars and me. He's already so upset that his good friend, Arne, is too humiliated by Roland to come to the lodge."

"Just like Olga. Arne is Roland's father and she his wife, but they have no control over Roland's deeds. Arne is a good man, and this must be difficult for him, I'm sure," Dagmar said and kissed her husband goodbye.

There was a knock on the front door at half past seven later that night. Dagmar opened the door. "Olga, my God. What has happened?" Her hair was matted with blood and there were bruises covering her face. Dagmar screamed for George and knelt, almost too frightened to touch Olga for fear she might hurt her even more.

Olga raised her hand, nearly too weak to speak. "Roland hurt me," she mumbled and fainted into Dagmar's lap.

George came when he heard the commotion and lifted Olga in his arms.

"Take her upstairs. I'll call Lars." Dagmar's heart pounded as she connected with the operator and rang Lars. "Hurry, Lars," she pleaded with her brother. Dagmar had seen this ruthless kind of beating before. It had nearly killed her only friend Lili, and now she feared for her only remaining sister's life.

Minutes ticked by that felt like hours. Lars had immediately sent Ellen to call for Dr. Jensen, which only heightened Dagmar's fears. She wrung her hands again and again, silently praying for her sister. How had they let this happen? Olga wasn't strong like Lili. Please God, let her survive, Dagmar prayed.

Lars came downstairs and into the front parlor where all

the family had gathered. His look was somber. "She's resting now and will need lots of assistance for some time. Her jaw is broken."

Mamma and Dagmar gasped as Ellen stepped to their side.

Lars continued. "She has several broken ribs and numerous lacerations. I called Dr. Jensen to assist because she is also expecting a baby, and they are both in danger."

"With child? My poor baby." Mamma sobbed as Papa hugged her tightly.

"Olga will need to stay here and heal. She's taken quite a beating and will need someone to look after her," Lars said.

"We'll all do our best," Regina said placing her hand on Helga's shoulder. "Family takes care of family. Let's try not to worry."

The hours would tick on, and so would the days before Olga showed signs of improvement. Dagmar sat next to her sister trying to cheer her up. "I've brought you fresh lilacs."

Olga strained to smile through the pain in her jaw. "Lilacs were Myrtle's favorite flower. I remember how she loved them."

"I know, but the roses haven't bloomed yet for you," Dagmar said. "When they do, I shall bring you a whole bush to fill the room," she laughed, immediately regretting making Olga smile again.

"Where is Roland?" Olga asked.

Dagmar remained silent for a moment trying to reel in her anger. It wouldn't do to upset Olga anymore. "He's disappeared. They think he has gone deep into the forest, somewhere on the reservation land. He thinks he's safer there, because the sheriff can't pursue him on Indian land, but he can't hide there forever," she said.

"I don't care what happens to him. I just don't want him near me or my child ever again." Olga turned her head and stared out the window.

Dagmar knew there would be no comforting her sister on this day. She recalled that look of hopelessness, fear, and helplessness. Staring out a window, looking for any sign that this was not your destiny. Dagmar shut the bedroom door and let her sister rest to grow stronger. She was out of physical danger from Roland, but Dagmar knew those scars would run deep for a very long time.

The next night, an enormous explosion was heard outside of town and a fireball was seen for miles. Hauling trucks and the remnants of a still operation were scattered about, burnt and mangled from the explosion.

Marvin, along with four other unknown men were found charred and unrecognizable, lying in the dirt. Roland's flask with his name engraved in fancy letters was found mixed in the rubble. To everyone's great shock, the burned and bloody body of Arne, Roland's father, was found near the edge of the clearing. Everyone speculated it must have been he who had set the explosion into motion. He had been stabbed and then somehow tried to flee moments before the explosion killed him.

Dagmar sat at the table where she once sat as a child. She tended Papa's hands. Gently spreading the ointment she had taken from Lars, who now stood staring out the window with Ellen at his side. George sat in the chair with his jacket torn and smelling of smoke and mud.

"What happened?" Dagmar asked.

George looked at his wife. "We went to the forest to reason with Roland. Arne begged your papa, Lars, and me to let him speak with his son first. We stayed further back to allow him time to see what he could do. I don't know. Suddenly there was a struggle. Arne ran, but there was an explosion. There was nothing we could do for Arne or any of the others, but we thought it best to get out of there." George sighed.

Nothing further was said from that night on. Roland and Arne were dead. Regina's words would forever echo in Dagmar's mind. What would you do to protect your family?

Chapter 30

"Good morning, Myrtle," Dagmar said as she placed a new bundle of flowers in the vase next to Myrtle's headstone. A chilly wind blew, and she tightened her coat. "Looks like it's going to be a cold winter, so I'll have to be talking to you in my prayers until spring. Papa is hoping a good snow cover will help the farmers from all this terrible drought and dust storms," she said brushing away the fallen leaves and twigs from a distant tree. Placing her woolen blanket on the cold ground, she settled in to fill her twin sister in on all the latest news.

"Mr. Roosevelt, the new President, certainly is shaking things up. We sit by the radio for his fireside chats and hope for better times. He said the only thing we must fear is fear itself, but these are frightening times, I tell you Myrtle. He closed all the banks for a holiday. It lasted four days. Thousands of banks have failed. George said it was the only way to stop all the runs on the bank. I worry for him, but I guess I worry for all of us." Dagmar shifted on the blanket to get more comfortable.

"They're going to end prohibition soon. Roland would have been furious." She spit on the ground, in the opposite direction of her sister's grave. "May that devil Rest in Peace. Olga is doing much better, now that the twins were born safe and healthy. Mamma says they look just like the two of us and will keep Olga on her toes." Dagmar laughed.

"We had fun when we're growing up, Myrtle. I can't believe you've been gone twelve years." She sighed and was quiet for a moment. Shaking her sadness away, she continued, "I don't remember if I told you before, when she packed her belongings to move in with Mamma and Papa, Olga found Roland's hidden stash of money. It was a lot and at least she and the girls won't have to worry about their future."

Dagmar continued. "Lars and Ellen are happy with their little boy, and they're starting a clinic to help others who are too poor to come into town. I think our brother is the kindest of all of us, and Ellen is perfect for him," she said.

"I have to get home soon, but I wanted to let you know Mamma and Papa are well, and Auntie Hilda is fine as well. Mamma doesn't walk anymore, and Papa has grown very serious since all that happened with Roland. I'm so sorry you weren't here. Maybe together, we could have protected Olga, but at least she has her beautiful little girls now."

The wind blew again, and Dagmar knew it was time to go. She leaned in close and whispered to her sister, "Don't worry about me. George was the true prince. He's a good man and fine father to our boys. We're still searching for Marta, but I am happy." She rose with a smile, taking her blanket with her. "I love you, Myrtle," she said as she turned to walk home to her family.

The winter had proven not to be that bad, nor even the

next one, but the howling winds of the dust bowl continued to strip the lands of the Great Plains for the next two years. Some families pushed west to California, while others made do and prayed for better times. The weekly papers brought photographs and stories of the plight of the very poor around the country. These were difficult times. Social unrest rattled in the corners of America. Unions were formed and the government grasped at every straw to put the unemployed back to work and aid the needy, but the task would not be easy or quick.

For days and weeks, Dagmar watched and worried as Papa seemed less and less interested in the dealership. "Papa, we need to go over the books for this quarter. The new government contracts have improved our profitability," Dagmar said as she sat down in the chair across from her father's at his desk. She hoped today would be the day they could make their plans for the future. "I think we need to hire a new parts manager. Demand is up, and although Roland wasn't the best manager, there is a need for someone, at least part time."

Papa tapped his pencil on the desk and said, "Yes there is, but we need to talk."

Dagmar didn't like his serious tone. "What's wrong?"

"There is nothing wrong," he said sitting back in his chair. "You've done a fine job getting things in order and keeping it running after the accident. I'm very proud of you."

Dagmar stared at father and could feel his pain. The burns and scars on his hands had healed, but he clearly was not the same from that night on. "Thank you," she said. "The new contracts have helped, but I'm not sure how long it's going to be before people can afford new cars again. I was wondering if you had any ideas."

Papa leaned forward and folded his hands together. "I think we should sell the dealership," he said.

"We're just starting to make a good profit, and I can help more. I didn't mean to worry you. I'm sorry," Dagmar said, feeling alarmed and confused.

"No. No. You've been a big help, but Arne and I started this together. He let Roland talk him into stepping aside, but we both knew that was a problem. Arne had hoped Roland would find his way and settle down. For generations our men owned land, farms, and businesses. They passed from father to son. It is not easy for us to change what has always been for us. Lars did not want the farm, the store or even this dealership. Now he is a fine doctor. Thankfully the Lord blessed me with a very capable daughter to help me, but I'm tired and it is time to let it go and think about the future," Papa said.

"I know things have been hard, but are you sure this is what you want?" Dagmar said.

"Yes. There have been more letters from home and not just from Norway. The Depression was very hard in Europe and beyond. Even harder than here. The politics are getting more and more rash and dangerous. Hitler has taken over the Rhineland, Spain is being ripped apart by a civil war, and Italy has a new monster in Mussolini," Papa sighed.

Dagmar had listened to the radio and read the same articles but had hoped the problems of Europe would stay far away from Minaka Falls and her family.

"The United States wants no part in the coming war, but we

160

may have no choice," Papa said. When your neighbor's house and fields burn, you can't turn away, or soon your house and fields will burn. I had a visit from someone representing some very influential people about increasing production at the mine. If war comes, there will be a need for the raw materials to manufacture tanks, ships, planes, and munitions even if the United States never enters the war. Like it or not, I think that is the future, not far away," he said frowning.

Dagmar sat calmly taking in all that her father had said. If he was right, to run the dealership would be too much. "Have you had any offers to buy it?" she asked.

He responded with a simple yes, and Dagmar knew his mind was made up.

"I think it is for the best," her father said.

"Papa, do you ever feel like we're just watching our lives through a window? Things are happening and you can't stop them, no matter how much you try or pray?" she asked.

He thought for a moment before speaking. "Yes, I suppose it feels that way sometimes. I know you are talking about Myrtle. I remember that day you watched through the window when she died."

Tears welled in Dagmar's eyes, and she knew he understood her.

"There was nothing you could have done. Nothing any of us could have done. Now, well over a decade later, they have new medicines, so others don't have to suffer and lose their loved ones as we did. You know Lars stood beside you that day and felt just as helpless. Watching poor Myrtle and seeing how it affected Mamma is why he became a doctor. It is how he survived that day. The world is a window through which we see many bad things happening that shape us. I felt that

161

way when I watched Olv wither away and when Arne tried to stop Roland. It's how we choose to move forward that is up to us. You're young, Dagmar, but have had to endure a number of harsh things, and there will be more to come. My sad and lost little girl is a wise and kind woman now. You've built a good family, and you work very hard here. When we expand the mine, I want you to be in charge," Papa said.

"In charge? But I'm a woman," she said, looking stunned.

"I'm aware of that," Papa said with a wink. "In case you haven't noticed, women are very capable. They run companies, households, countries, and empires. You, my dear, are just as capable. The foreman at the mine is doing a good job and understands the needs of the workers. We'll have to make some improvements as well. When the mines first opened, they were manned by immigrants of many sorts who were anxious to have a job at any cost. They didn't speak English and were taken advantage of. Now, there are second and third generations who are forming unions to protect themselves. My brother understood this and did his best, but it's still a dangerous hard life," Papa said.

"Do you think they will be a problem?" she asked, wondering if she were up to this task.

"I think we were immigrants not so long ago, and we know how difficult such a life is. After the last war, the mines began to close. Many owners couldn't pay the high taxes. There are several good men out there who would be ready to help us expand. I've got a young man from Hibbing coming in, pending your approval. He could manage the day-to-day operation, while you and I make ready for what is to come. We cannot just stand and watch through this window as our neighbors' fields burn. No, as the world burns," he added with tears in his eyes.

Dagmar stood up, uncertain if she should shake her father's hand to seal the deal or not. He was entrusting her with everything he had built and that which his brother had built as well.

Papa put out his hand toward her, and she shook it as he pulled her in close. "We are family," he said hugging her tightly. "If we stick together, we can do anything we set our minds to. We must hope for better times."

Chapter 31

Dagmar shuffled around the papers on her desk and tried not to let the exhaustion get the best of her. Her father was entrusting their entire future in her every decision, but George had been right. The mine was a disaster. Uncle Ervin and his son had barely scratched the surface of the mine, so there was a great deal of promise and possibility, but at what cost remained to be seen.

The door to the mine office creaked open and a puff of red iron dust permeated behind the tall man from Hibbing as he sauntered in. Dagmar scrutinized his every step forward. His dress was neat, but not too formal. That was good, she thought. He would have to command respect from the men, but not give the appearance of being too far above them. He was obviously physically fit, which was essential to traverse the mines, whether they be underground or the massive pits. So far, so good.

"You're late, Mr. Morgan," Dagmar said sternly.

"My apologies, Mrs. Hanson." He extended a firm handshake

and offered no explanation. After quickly releasing her hand, he pulled a nearby chair up in front of Dagmar's desk in one swift motion. Getting straight down to business, he asked, "Now tell me, what's the state of our mine?"

Dagmar was far too tired to wrestle with the usual how-do-you-dos and small talk. She decided to follow his lead. After all, as manager of the mine, it would be essential. She did just that from here out.

She had checked out his background. Morgan was raised in the North Hibbing mine town just thirty miles to the north. His father had been a foreman, but young Theodore "Ted" Morgan had shown great promise in school and had left the area to secure further education.

Leaving the area was not unusual. The Iron Range had once been a wild paradise of clear lakes and sprawling forests of white pines for as far as the eye could see. Overzealous logging had stripped the land straight to the Canadian border in less than a generation and mining left huge pits and pocks scarring the land throughout the range. The mines once employed twelve thousand men but had reduced down to a couple of thousand after the Great War and the Depression had seen the continuation of mine closings.

Times were changing and Dagmar was certain the renewed threat of war in Europe would once again increase demand for ore and would call men back to the mines. There were over a hundred and twenty separate mines on the range, most owned by the big names of Pillsbury, Merritt, and Rockefeller.

Two Brothers mine, as it had become to be known, was a small operation compared to most, but Dagmar was determined to change that, and she knew the dashingly good-looking Mr. Morgan had the skills to get the job done.

Others had recognized his talent and drive. Upon returning home, mine management embraced his knowledge of new techniques and readiness to accept modern mechanization over the old slower traditional axe-and-shovel methods, which would increase their production and profitability.

Mr. Morgan had a certain charm and wit, and combined, they quickly gained him a name. What wasn't expected was the whisper of scandal that followed that charm and wit. Involvement with a certain young daughter of one of the owners resulted in his banishment from the long reach of their operations. Dagmar was the only woman at the mine and she and George were unshakable. She would have to trust him to expand the mine and herself to get the money needed to do just that.

"We're in great shape, Mr. Morgan." Dagmar said holding her head high.

"Call me Ted," he responded. "Let's see if we can make that statement come true."

"Call me Dagmar. And we will."

Dagmar hadn't been home for dinner in days, and long workdays turning into late nights was beginning to become a habit. Most of the lights in the house were out and a covered cold plate waited for her in the refrigerator when she finally arrived. It was quiet in the kitchen as she sat, amazed how much things had changed, even in the Depression.

The refrigerator kept their food cold and fresh. The electric stove was far safer and heated up quicker than the old gas ones, and certainly no one missed the endless hauling and chopping to keep Mamma's cast-iron stove fed.

What she did miss was Mamma's fresh cinnamon buns and the aroma of good dark coffee. She couldn't remember the last time she had prepared or even sat and enjoyed a meal with her family. Harold was growing up so fast. He was the spitting image of his father and had all the same qualities she loved in George. Jimmy was turning into quite a wonder. Gone was the raggedy and scrawny little boy who had followed her around those first few days at the mine like a lost puppy. Dagmar sighed and knew she had best get to bed before the sun came calling her out of it again.

Slipping into the bed, the sheets felt cool and inviting. Her hair was still damp, and a slight shiver tingled across her body. A warm bath had been a delight to wash away the dust that followed everyone from the mine. Here in town few knew of the lives of those a mere twenty minutes away. She laid her head on the soft feathered pillow, determined to let tomorrow's worries rest where they were. Closing her eyes, she felt her husband's gentle kiss.

"I've been waiting for you, my love." George whispered in her ear as he inched closer.

Dagmar smiled uncertain why she deserved such a man. "You waited for me?"

"I'll always wait for you," he said kissing her tenderly.

"I'm so exhausted," she said rolling on her stomach as an obvious hint for her husband to massage her aching muscles. "I'm worried I'm neglecting all of you too much. We've hired a new manager, so I'm hoping that will lighten the load, but there seems so much to do and not enough time to do it."

George kneaded his fingers over her shoulders trying to ease the stressful knots away. Easing the ones of self-doubt would take a little longer. "Dagmar, your papa chose you to lead the way because he knew who you were. Now you just need to see who you are. Sometimes it takes you a minute to get your feet steady and find your way, but once you do, there's no stopping you. We're all happy and love you. Don't doubt that, or yourself," he said.

Dagmar moaned as his words and touch began to work their way through her mind and body. His hands were large and strong, yet so gentle and enticing. She moaned again and gone were the problems of the day. Tomorrow she would be the newest titan of the Minnesota mining world, but tonight, hmmm….

Tonight, she belonged to the man she loved who also loved her.

Chapter 32

D
agmar rose the next morning feeling rested and rejuvenated. The house was quiet except for a muffled stirring in the kitchen. She crept down the stairs, certain no one would possibly be awake at this early hour. Peeking in the door she was astonished to see Caroline sitting at the large breakfast table in the center of the kitchen.

"Morning," Caroline whispered as she motioned her in.

"Goodness," Dagmar said. "What are you doing up so early?"

"I'm always first up. Making the morning bread and the first pot of coffee long before anyone else rises gives me pleasure. I like the quiet and the feeling of my family sleeping peacefully in their beds, all safe and sound. The day is never more perfect."

Dagmar smiled, thinking how that was so true and wondered if this had been Caroline's routine when George and Harry were young. She poured herself a cup of the strong, rich smelling coffee and added just a dab of cream.

"I'm sorry, I didn't know it was you who made this wonderful warm bread for us each morning," she said, wondering what other details she had begun to miss about her family.

"Mother does all the cooking. It makes her happy, and she really is a much better cook than I am," Carolina chuckled, "but I like to bake. The boys like my ginger cookies and you and George like the butter ones, when there is enough sugar ration."

"I love those little cookies. They're just like Mamma makes," Dagmar said.

"That's because your Mamma taught me to make them. I wanted you to be happy here, and George said they were your favorite, so I asked your mother for the recipe. About twice a month the two of us bake together and brag about our grandchildren at her house."

Dagmar was stunned. "I did not know you and Mamma were friends."

"Oh yes, and your Auntie Hilda stops by too, but just for tasting and gossiping. Without her, the two of us would have no idea what was going on in town. She keeps us up to date on who's courting who, who's wearing the newest fashions," she paused, looked around, and lowered her voice to a whisper before adding, "and whose husbands are stepping out."

"I'm so glad you and Regina agreed to stay here with us. I can't thank you enough for all you do, taking care of the boys and making this house such a warm and loving home. We'd starve if I were cooking, and there certainly wouldn't be any cookies," she jested before seeing the tears welling in Caroline's eyes. "I'm sorry. Did I upset you?" Dagmar reached for her mother-in-law's hand.

Caroline shook her head and wiped the tear from the corner of her eye. "I'm fine," she said, then paused. "Mother and my father always treated me as though I was perfect and could do no wrong. When I married Karl, he was the same, until we had the boys. George was the easy one, a lot like me. He learned early how to sidestep Karl's moods and unreasonable demands. Harry, on the other hand…." She trailed off, smiling and frowning all in the same moment. "He yielded to no one. A bit like mother, I'm afraid," she said. Her voice was filled with longing and pride. "I'm sorry for what Karl did to you and Harry. Most of all, I'm sorry we haven't found Marta yet."

Dagmar placed her hands on the table and tapped her fingers lightly against it, her eyes closed. It was a nervous habit she had had since she was a young child, whenever she was uncertain what to say next. Her eyes opened, and Dagmar spoke to Caroline with a newfound closeness. "I loved Harry, but we were young and did not know what lay ahead in the world for us. We were both lonely and in need of comfort. Harry is gone," she said. "But Marta was a gift of that love, and somehow, I'm certain she will come home to me one day. I know that sounds crazy, since there have been no clues where she is, but I can feel it in my heart. She's coming home."

"I'm so sorry." Caroline leaned forward and embraced her daughter-in-law.

Dagmar sat back and straightened her robe. "Let's not have any more regrets or apologies. We're blessed and have a fine home here together. George is a good man and a wonderful husband." She paused for a moment, thinking how for the first time she realized how much she really did love George and as twisted as her fate had been, George was her destiny. In this house that had once fostered so much pain and hurt, now grew love and joy. "We're happy, Caroline, and I hope you are too."

"Morning. Time to get some breakfast made for this hungry bunch," Regina announced, coming through the door, already dressed and ready for the day.

An hour and a half later, everyone was dressed and ready to face the day. "I'll drop the boys off at school on my way to the bank," George said before gathering his satchel of papers he had so meticulously worked on last night. "It will give us a few extra minutes together."

"I'm going to let Jimmy play hooky today and go with me. I don't think I've spent nearly enough time with him lately. Things have been so busy at the mine, and I'm excited to show him all the improvements we've made. I'm afraid Harold is still coughing and sneezing, so you're on your own today," Dagmar said.

"All boys need to play hooky once in a while," George said. "I wish I could join you, but I will be seeing you later. Remember, I'm coming out to the mine before the end of the day. The paperwork for the new equipment loan is nearly complete, but it's likely to be around lunchtime or so. Maybe I'll play hooky with you two this afternoon," he said before he kissed her goodbye.

"Where's Dad?" Jimmy said, rushing down the stairs. "I'm ready to go."

He dresses and grooms like a miniature version of George, but with a little roughness around the edges, Dagmar thought. "You're taking the day off today and going back to the mine with me. No school. Just us," she said, turning and grabbing her satchel of paperwork. "Let's get going. I don't want to be late."

The ride out to the mine had been rocky at best. Jimmy sat mostly looking out the window as they meandered the back roads past the lake, several farms, and through the forests and finally neared the mine. Dagmar had tried but failed at every turn to strike up a conversation with her young son. She thought he was happy and growing more and more comfortable living with them every day, but today he just wasn't himself.

"You should see the new clinic your Uncle Lars and Aunt Ellen have set up for the miners and their families. There're all kinds of new equipment there, so everyone can be treated, just like in Minaka Falls. You are never going to believe this. Aunt Olga, who hated school herself, has made all sorts of improvements in the school. She set up a little library and everything. I think you're really going to like it," she said.

"I can be better. I don't need any more clothes, and I'll stop taking extra food. I promise," Jimmy said, bursting into tears.

Dagmar eased the car up next to the mine office. Shut off the ignition and pulled the handbrake. She studied the young fragile boy for just a minute before speaking. For all his rough, tough, 'I can take care of myself' facade, he was just a little boy.

"What is all this?" she said, taking him into her arms.

"I thought you liked me, and I thought you wanted me to live with you and take care of Harold. I can do better. I promise," he pleaded again.

It had been an eventful morning. First Caroline, which warmed her heart, and now sweet Jimmy. "You don't have to be better, Jimmy," she said handing him one of her embroidered handkerchiefs from her new pocketbook, a birthday present from George. "You are perfect. I want you to eat all the food you want, and Harold is your brother. You are to watch out for him, like a big brother should, but it is your father's and my job to take care of both of you."

"I thought you were bringing me back, that you didn't love me anymore," he said.

"I love you so much that I wanted to show you off, and I wanted you to see how much things have changed. The mine is just starting to do a lot better, and I don't want anyone ever to be living in a shed again."

Dagmar brushed his straight brown hair back in order and decided he was old enough to know about Marta. "I'm going to share a little secret with you. It's a secret only our family knows, except Harold. He's too young," she said. She told him she once shared a shed with her best friend long ago, and he has a sister named Marta who lives far away but will come home one day. "Remember, this is a secret that only our family knows. You are and will always be my son, and you are a huge blessing to our family. If you never want to come back to the mine again, you don't have to. You are my son, and I will protect you forever."

Jimmy lunged into her embrace. "Thank you, Mamma. Thank you. I love you and don't worry, I'll always protect you, too." They sat in silence, hugging a little longer before they got out of the car and began what Dagmar hoped would be a quiet day at the mine together.

Chapter 33

Ted stepped out onto the mine porch and shut the door behind him. He pushed his hair back from his face and shook his head in frustration. Dagmar approached the porch wondering what had her new mine manager looking so frazzled and worn. So much for a quiet day, she thought.

"Is there a problem?" Dagmar asked.

"A big one," Ted said now appearing more annoyed than worried. "Your sister Olga came to drop a few things off for you. She's got the other ladies in the office in a tizzy, and they've left for the day. I tried to reason with her. I don't want any more trouble, but if I stay in there any longer, I'm likely to be engaged."

Dagmar patted Ted on the shoulder, smiled and shook her head.

"I understand. She's Olga. Leave this to me. Could you do me a favor and show my young assistant some of the improvements we've made?" She put her arm tenderly around Jimmy making certain he was okay with going without her.

"He's taken the day off from school but is very smart just like his father and is eager to help. Give me a few minutes with our Olga. She's a handful, but I'll do my best. Then I'll come join you two."

"Thank you, ma'am," Ted said looking relieved.

"Dagmar, please," she said grinning. She may be happily married, but she was a long way off from ma'am in her book. Stepping forward and opening the door, it was now time to deal with the likes of her ever-so-entertaining sister. God, help her.

Olga sat in Dagmar's chair behind her desk, filing a nail and humming "You Must Have Been a Beautiful Baby" along with Bing Crosby on the radio. Dagmar couldn't help but notice she was wearing what looked to be yet another gorgeous new outfit. A powdered baby blue knit dress snuggly wrapped itself around her every curve. She accented it with a single strand of white pearls and a turned-up ostrich feathered hat. She must have been quite a challenge for the stunning, handsome Mr. Morgan. Dagmar chuckled. Ted was correct to be cautious. Olga's charms were endless.

"Morning, big sister. Love the new addition to the office."

"Do you, now?" Dagmar said with her arms crossed tapping her foot. "You about scared the wits out of him, and we had a lot of work to get done in this office today."

Olga gave a little pout and started humming again.

"Oh no, you don't. Olga Marie, you have upended my entire day before it has even begun. I could just wring your neck,"

Dagmar said.

Olga laughed. "Maybe you could get the handsome one to do it for you. He has such big strong hands." She spun around in Dagmar's chair appearing as if she had not a care in the world.

"Get out of my chair," Dagmar demanded with her hands on her hips. She walked over to the desk and pulled her sister up into her arms embracing her in a warm welcome. "I love you baby sister, but must you be so bold?"

"Bold? He's a fine-looking man and I think he likes me," she said adjusting her new hat. "Besides, you have a good-looking husband. Why shouldn't I?"

They both laughed together, thankful the days of conflict and misunderstandings were behind them. Dagmar was happy to see her sister well and smiling again. Roland's death and the birth of her daughters had taken a lot out of her. Olga had done her best to be a good wife to Roland, but now the bruises of that marriage were just beginning to heal.

"Olga, it's been less than a year since—" She stopped herself when she saw the shadow come over her sister's face. "I'm sorry. Really, I am. But I want you to take your time and take care of yourself and your girls. You fall in love so easily and I don't want you hurt ever again."

"Good heavens, Dagmar! I just met the man. You act like we're getting engaged. You have such an imagination," she said, laughing. "But do you think he likes me?"

"Olga," Dagmar said before she saw a look of panic on her sister's face. She had turned pale white and steadied herself on the desk as she began to tremble. "Olga," Dagmar said feeling panicked as well. "What's wrong? You look like you've seen a ghost."

"Roland," Olga muttered. "It's Roland."

Dagmar tuned as the door of the office flung wide open. Her knees went weak, and she gasped in shock. "We thought you were dead," she murmured. "Everyone thinks you are dead."

"Not quite, dear sister-in-law. As usual, you don't know everything," Roland sneered.

"What do you want?" Dagmar sneered back.

"We'll get to that," he said, grinning. "But first, no hugs for your long-lost husband, Olga?"

Olga stumbled back and Dagmar reached for her and guided her into the chair sitting next to her desk. She turned back to Roland, filled with hate and anger. The memories of the day Olga lay beaten on her doorstep were fresh in her memory. "You leave her alone."

Roland flashed the gun he had been hiding. "You're not in charge here. We're going to do what I say to do. First thing, I want my money, and I want it now."

Dagmar saw his look was fierce and uncompromising. She willed herself not to show the fear that was running rampant deep inside her. She stood up to Marvin and she would stand up to Roland and try to forget he had a gun pointed at them. "That money belongs to Olga and your daughters," she said.

Roland's expression was unmoved at the mention of his family.

"It's my money, and I want it," Roland said.

"You can't have it!" Olga shouted. "It was ill-gotten money and you almost killed me and our daughters. I won't give it to you."

"We'll see about that, dear spoiled Olga. I told you I never wanted any brats like you. I even gave you money to get rid of it. But you just don't listen, do you, Olga?" Roland stepped closer and raised the gun higher, pointing it directly at Olga.

"Stop!" Dagmar shouted, raising one hand to protect Olga and one to stop Roland. "The money isn't here and there's no way we can get it without causing suspicion," she said trying to calm Roland.

"Suspicion? They all think I'm dead. I want my money," he said, cocking the gun.

"The money was put in the bank and Papa controls how much she gets. Olga was too sick to handle anything for a long time. Papa won't give it to you," Dagmar said gritting her teeth.

"You bitches are going to die, then."

"Wait. There's money in the safe. You can have that. It's almost as much as Olga has. It's the mine payroll and money for a large new piece of equipment we're buying. Take it and leave!" Dagmar shouted.

Roland appeared to be thinking and weighing his options. "Empty that satchel and get me the money," he said, pointing to Dagmar's bag. "Fill it and be quick about it."

Dagmar moved to the safe, and her hands shook as she turned the dial one number and then the next and the next, until the door opened. Stacks of cash were neatly wrapped and divided, waiting for today's payroll distribution. She took each stack and placed them one by one into the satchel and then handed the bag to Roland.

"That's better," he said before he heard a car door shut outside. He peered through the window as Dagmar and Olga froze.

"Oh God, it's George," Dagmar said. "Please Roland, just go."

Roland stepped to the side of the door and warned them to be silent.

George walked in, shut the door behind him and felt an immediate blow to the head before staggering to his knees. He braced his hand on the floor, twisted around, sat up and looked with shock at Roland. Dagmar rushed to his side.

"Enough of that," Roland said. "Get back by your sister."

"He's hurt, you bastard," Dagmar said refusing to move.

"He's fine. We're all going on a little trip. Get him up and you keep your hands where I can see them. I've got something to show you. No funny business, or we'll end this right here."

Dagmar wasn't sure what Roland had planned but knew it couldn't be good. She prayed someone might rescue them but had a bad feeling this wasn't going to end well. They all moved to the door and headed out with Roland clearly in charge.

God help us, she thought.

Chapter 34

Ted grumbled as he kicked the red dirt and marched his way closer to the new mineshaft.

"So, now I'm a damn babysitter. Bad enough a man can't just do his job without women nagging him all the time," he mumbled.

"I don't like girls either," Jimmy announced, kicking his share of the dirt. "There's this one girl at school who keeps trying to get me to kiss her. When I didn't, she told the teacher I was mean to her. You know, I used to live here," he jabbered on, suddenly changing the subject. "See that shed? Right there. Sure got cold in the winter."

"I thought Mrs. Hanson was your mother," Ted said, looking confused.

"She is now, and I have a brother, too. Mamma says we have a sister, too, who lives far away from here, but is coming home one day."

"Is that right?" Ted said, allowing his new young friend to prattle on.

"Mamma is great, and don't worry about Aunt Olga. She's really nice, but she has had a hard time, Mamma says." His eyes lit up. "She was married to a bad man. He was a whiskey runner and blew up his still and almost the whole Indian reservation. I sure would have liked to have seen that. POW!" He jumped up waving his arms about. "The bad guy is dead now, but he really hurt Aunt Olga before that happened. They thought she was going to die. Do you think I could drive that big shovel lifter one day?"

"Let's settle down here and get some work done," Ted said, trying not to laugh. The boy had an imagination as big as the sky and changed the subject like the wind.

Ted spent the next two hours showing young Jimmy around and pointing out what had recently been major improvements for the workers.

"Your mother insisted we get things in shape, making sure the living conditions for each family met her standards before we cut the new shaft," Ted said. He hadn't understood her logic at the time and sensed there was even more he needed to learn about his new boss. She was quite an amazing woman, but he was going to have to watch out for that sister.

"Who's working at the old shaft now?" Jimmy asked.

"Nobody. Dynamite's been laid and we're waiting for a new piece of equipment to arrive before we let her blow."

"What? Why are you blowing it up?" Jimmy asked.

"The main entrance is no longer big enough to handle all the men and gear we're going to need to increase production. This was a small mine that really had barely scratched the surface of its potential. I'm going to help your grandpa and mother change that," Ted said.

The two mine openings were on opposite ends of the town,

and it was a healthy walk back towards the main office, which was by the original shaft. Jimmy had enjoyed his return to the mine, but he stopped abruptly.

"What's wrong?" Ted said.

"Shush," Jimmy said, grabbing Ted's hand and pulling behind one of the old outbuildings.

"Hey kid, I've got lots of work to get done. You need to quit playing around."

"I'm not playing. That's the bad guy." Jimmy pointed to four people going into the mouth of the old mine.

Ted wasn't sure what was going on but was certain it couldn't be good. "I thought you said he was dead," Ted said.

"A bunch of people blew up, but they said he was blown to smithereens. Guess he got away, and it looks like he has a gun," Jimmy said.

Ted liked this less and less, but there was no time to delay. "You stay here, kid. I'm going to get the shotgun from the office. On second thought, you run back to the new mine and get some help. Hurry!"

Now inside the mine, Dagmar was certain they were in deep trouble. They all stopped just inside the entrance. Olga trembled, still clutching the satchel of money Roland had forced her to carry.

"Drop the bag right there and light the torch, then hand it to me," Roland commanded. He watched as Olga narrowed her eyes but did as he said when he waved the gun in warning. He then held his gun steady in one hand and raised the torch to illuminate the dark cavern. "Now, we're all going to go in until I say stop," Roland said.

The mine had been emptied only a week earlier. All the dynamite had been carefully placed to cause the maximum destruction. They were waiting on the newly available Primacord, which made detonating safer. Roland had obviously been there for the last couple of nights, hiding and waiting for his chance to strike. A new path of the less-stable black powder trailed back into the mine.

"You won't get away with this," George said.

"Shut up! You're not with all your Mason buddies now!" Roland shouted. "I saw you that night. You and your buddies come to burn me out. I saw you," Roland said.

"We didn't come to burn you out. Your father thought he could convince you to do the right thing."

"That's a lie. I saw you and Christianson. I bet all the Seven and the Masons were there trying to steal what was mine."

"It was just us three, but that was a mistake. You killed him, didn't you?" George said in a low calm voice.

"That was his fault!" Roland shouted. "The old fool pulled a knife on me and thought he could force me to go back. When that didn't work, he said he'd kill me before I shamed him and his family anymore, then he lunged at me. I had no choice. He got what he deserved. Now you're going to get what you deserve. I'm going to blow up your livelihood and old man Christianson's precious family. The Seven and the Masons can go to hell!"

"My God, you killed Arne?" Dagmar was stunned and knew time was running out.

She and George looked at one another. They could rush him, but more than likely a stray bullet would set the whole place

184

up into one big explosion. They couldn't take that chance.

"Don't anybody move!" Ted shouted. He pointed the gun straight at Roland.

Roland grabbed Dagmar and held her as a shield in front of him, dropping the torch to the ground, and causing a momentary confusion. George lunged forward, pushing Roland back and dragging Dagmar as they all began to run except Roland, lying on the ground, staring at the sizzling path racing to the back of the mine chamber.

The explosion rumbled, and the ground shook. Rocks and debris blasted out of the mine opening knocking everyone to the ground.

Ted and Olga had gotten the furthest, but lay huddled next to a large tree. "Help!" he yelled as Olga screamed at the sight of the blood gushing from his head. "Settle down, woman. It's just a little cut," Ted said, wincing in pain.

"It's not a little cut, and don't call me woman. You know full well my name is Olga."

"Mamma!" Jimmy screamed rushing from behind a huge rock, where he and the other miners had taken cover when they felt the first rumble begin in a succession of other larger blasts. Dagmar and George lay together, motionless, covered in gravel and dust. Jimmy ran, falling to his knees, franticly brushing away the top layer of gravel and dust. "Mamma, daddy, please don't die! Please don't die!" he screamed.

One of the other miners pulled him back as the others turned first Dagmar and then George over. Each moaned in unison and reached for the other's hand once again.

"I'm fine," Dagmar said, lying still.

George reached his other hand out. "We're okay, son. We're okay," he said, pulling Jimmy into their embrace.

Ted and Olga were helped over to the happy family. Olga hugged them all and sighed with relief as she thanked them all for not bleeding. "I hate blood," she said. Pausing for a moment, she stood up and took a deep breath. "Did Roland make it out?"

Dagmar watched the trembling, fearful look in her sister's eyes. She knew Olga had both loved and loathed Roland. He had been her husband and the father of her children, but ultimately, had almost killed all of them. "I'm sorry. He's gone," was the best she could say.

"Are you sure?" Olga sighed.

"We're sure," Ted stepped forward and spoke. "We're not going to let anyone hurt you again," he said putting a protective arm around her middle, holding her close.

Dagmar looked at George who smiled and winked, just once, telling her he too knew Olga would be just fine and that they were probably going to be seeing Ted around a whole lot more.

Chapter 35

Dagmar sat next to the window enjoying the quiet hush of the early morning perched high above in the cozy warmth of her bedroom. A light dusting of fresh snow had begun its arrival just before dawn. Minaka Falls was a picture of perfection, that one perfect moment where nature lay undisturbed by the motion of the day. She took a deep breath, thankful for the time to reflect. She and Papa had agreed the mine would be closed today and for the next three days in celebration of Christmas.

The last two years were so busy there had been little time to sit and enjoy. At long last, the Depression was finally ending, and the mine was producing an astronomical amount of iron ore. The two main shafts were going deeper and deeper every day and the new surface pit had far exceeded everyone's expectations. Papa was right, they were going to need the raw materials for steel, but it wasn't new cars that the world was demanding.

Last September, Hitler had marched into Poland and within

two days Great Britain and France had declared war, thus throwing all of Europe and Russia into the bowels of hell once again. The U.S. had signed a declaration of neutrality, pledging not to send their young men into the conflict, but just this last week, the Lend-Lease Act had been enacted.

Papa had been right, yet again. Europe was burning and something needed to be done. President Roosevelt had called for the production of new planes, ships, and other tools of war. The country would remain out of the conflict, but we would not stand and watch our neighbor's house burn any longer.

Dagmar touched the cold windowpane, and a chill ran down her spine. Her mind and heart longed to slip back to her childhood so many years ago. But gone were the lush green forest brimming with the huge white pines. Crystal blue lakes to fish in the summer and skate on in the winter were now surrounded by towns and the ravaged landscape created by the giant mining pits.

So much had changed since the day she as a young girl and stood hiding in the background listening to her father bid farewell to his dear friend. She, like him, pledged to always protect her family. With her hand still on the window, she remembered the afternoon when the sun was warm and the lilacs bloomed, but no matter how hard she pleaded and prayed neither she nor anyone else could protect her family or sweet Myrtle. She had failed. When Marta and Lili had vanished without a clue, she had once again pleaded and prayed, but failed.

Dagmar raised her chin and swiped away her tears. She hadn't failed. George and she had a loving beautiful family. They had been blessed with their boys and a generous growing extended family. The family's wealth had grown as well, thanks to a lot of hard work and the prosperity of the mines. They would want for nothing, she thought. Nothing, she thought again. Myrtle was gone. It had taken her years to accept.

But Marta's disappearance was something she could not accept. Today was Christmas Eve, and she would have to try her best. Her family deserved that, she thought, as she glanced out the window. The truck delivering the daily milk puttered by with a barking dog trailing behind, ending the picture of perfection. It was time to set her thoughts aside and join her family. There were endless preparations to be made before the family gathered.

Cheer and excitement filled the house. The Christmas tree stood tall in the front window for all to know this was a house of joy and love. The multicolored lights were a delight, but George had mentioned perhaps they could tone down the tinsel a bit next year.

"Dagmar," Ellen said, walking up behind her. "Where am I supposed to put this platter full of more cookies? Your Mamma and Caroline have baked enough for the entire town. There's no more room." She turned and handed the dish to Dagmar.

"There's always room for more food if there is a Christianson in the house," she chuckled. "Olga and the girls should be here soon. I can't wait to hear how poor Ted the newlywed is surviving Olga and the twins. I'll bet they've kept him on his toes."

"Let's finish all this so we can enjoy everyone's company. Lars might be late. He's gone to an accident on the road coming into town," Ellen said.

"Oh, my goodness. George is traveling that road," Dagmar said, looking concerned.

"Lars said it was a family coming from out of town or at least that was what they said when a neighbor up the road called it in. One of the women was seriously hurt, so he may be awhile," Ellen sighed.

Another couple of hours ticked by and no sign of George or Lars. George had called to say he was at the hospital with Lars, and they would be there as soon as possible. He told her he had come across the accident and stopped to see if Lars needed any help. Dagmar didn't like the sound of his voice and thought perhaps it must have been a terrible sight.

"You have a beautiful home, Dagmar," Mamma said, trying to distract her daughter from her concerns. "The tree is perfect and never have I seen so many presents. We've been truly blessed with the treasures of family and the Lord's generosity to us. I know you're worried but am certain they'll be home safe and sound to you soon."

"I know they're safe, Mamma, but something has happened. I can't explain it. George was unsettled and I just don't know, but I feel it. Something has happened."

No sooner had she spoken her words and Harold shouted from the front foyer, "Dad and Uncle Lars are here! Let's open the presents!"

Dagmar looked at Mamma and was so relieved. All the awful scenarios that had run through her head were just plain silliness. Her family was home and now Christmas Eve could begin. It was the Norwegian way, she chuckled to herself.

Dagmar looked up and saw George and Lars standing in the doorway of the front parlor. In front of them were two young girls around fourteen years old or so. She studied the younger one's face, which somehow looked familiar, then glanced at the taller girl who looked nervous, but not frightened. Her face was slender and stunning, surrounded by soft flowing curls. Dagmar blinked her eyes and traced down her neck to a pendant, Myrtle's pendant. In an instant she knew, Marta was home.

George spoke first. "This is Marty," he said.

The young girl smiled and stepped forward. "Yes, I'm called Marty, but my real name is Marta Louisa Christianson, and this is my sister, Georgie. Her real name is Georgina, named after him." She pointed to George. "Who my Aunt Lili says is the bravest man she ever met, and I think you are our family," she said as boldly and confidently as Dagmar had ever seen Lili be.

"Lili," Dagmar whispered. "Yes, you are our family. We've been waiting for you." Dagmar jumped to her feet and crossed the room into her daughter's arms.

Marta hugged her mother tightly and then stepped back to explain. "Aunt Lili saw your picture in a magazine. She always told me one day I would come home to you. She wrote you a letter, but I guess you didn't get it yet. We drove a long way to be with you. She's hurt in the hospital, but Uncle Lars," she said, looking to Dagmar's brother for reassurance. "He said she'll be well and here with us in a few days."

Lars nodded in agreement.

"It's truly a Christmas miracle," Dagmar announced. She took her husband's arm, and they all settled in around the sparkling, tinsel explosion of a tree. Their family was complete, and they were blessed.

"Since it's a night of miracles," Lars said. "We'd like to make an announcement. We've been waiting to make sure all is well, but today we found out it's more than well. Ellen is having twins."

Olga laughed. "Well, I guess we might as well join in. I know we've only been married three months, but you know I don't like to be left behind. Let's just hope for Ted's sake we're not having twins as well."

Everyone laughed and hugged, filled with joy. Mamma cried and Papa raised a toast. "Skal. To the ever-growing and beloved Christianson family. May we forever cherish the treasure of our love, and each and every one of us."

Dagmar looked around her smiling, surrounded by children, husband, and family. She glanced out the window where fresh snow was fluttering down. This was destiny's window's perfect moment, beautiful and joyous. Come what may, they were blessed.

Epilogue

Winter, spring, summer, and fall had all come and gone across Minaka Falls and the Christianson family was once again preparing for the Christmas holidays. The new babies were napping, but the other young ones had gathered to assist in the baking. Mamma and Caroline headed the task force as they passed the aprons out and directed everyone to their appointed job.

"Not so much sugar, girls," Regina said. "There's still rationing going on," she added for good measure.

"We want them to be sweet, like you, Grams," Marta said, and giggled.

Dagmar was delighted when Regina's face lit up with pride. This was the happy home Regina had begged Dagmar to build so long ago. Dagmar and George's castle.

"Ja, it's wonderful," Papa said coming up behind her. "It's a good thing we have all done here. Ja, it is." He wrapped his arm around his eldest daughter.

"Let's just hope they don't burn down the kitchen," Dagmar

laughed.

"Nei. No," Papa corrected. "They're our new Seven. They'll stick together and can accomplish anything."

"I think you better count again. There's a few more than seven." She chuckled.

"Seven or a dozen, doesn't matter. It's knowing who they are and where they come from that matters. Each one is special and unique, but together growing from our past they will make a new path to the future. Ja, it is wonderful to see."

Dagmar glanced over the back doorway leading to the porch. There hung the old sign, Christianson with 'We The Seven' etched beneath it. She had snatched it in anger that day they all left the farm and kept it packed safely away. One day she showed George, who suggested they hang it over the back door. He said Papa would love it, but he had another sign made as well. We The Hansons hung just below it. She delighted in remembering him saying it was a good thing we had tall ceilings.

"Yes, Papa. It is a good thing," Dagmar said. "Come sit and I'll get you some good strong coffee so you can sample the cookies and breads."

"It is the Norwegian way," they both said and laughed together.

There was a sudden hush across the room when Mamma shushed them and turned the radio up. Most of the children were too young to know what was happening or what was about to happen.

"My God, they've attacked us," Papa said.

Mamma turned the radio off and asked Marta to take charge as the adults rushed to gather in the study around the big radio. "No need to frighten the children," Mamma said. "If grief and war are to come, there will be little enough time for them to know." She remembered back telling Hilda, her sister, almost the same words shortly before the diphtheria epidemic ravaged their family. "God help us," Mamma said.

Later, December 7th, the 'Day That Would Live in Infamy' was across every newspaper across the nation. No one knew what lay ahead, but as Papa once said, "Our neighbor's house is burning, now it is ours. God help us all," Mamma said once again. There would be no Christmas miracles this year.

About the Author

ROMANCE AUTHOR

JoLynn Kerr lives a wonderful life on the coastal Carolina beaches, which lends to the setting of many of her novels. She is surrounded by the love of her husband, children, grandchildren and extended family and friends who also inspire her endlessly. Having been a native of Charleston, SC for most of her life, she is deeply fascinated with how history, culture, and family impact us one generation to the next. No matter where you are in the perils of history, what your age or gender, we all strive for one destiny, to love and be loved. You can learn more about the author and her books at www.jolynnkerr.com.

Acknowledgments

I would like to express my gratitude and appreciation to the many who inspired and encouraged me along the way while completing this novel. First and always is my beloved sister, Karen, who will forever be my creative partner in almost every adventure of my life. May there be a million more.

Top of my list of thank you is my magical forever love, Bill. Always at my side, cheering me along. Through him and the love of our children, beautiful grandchildren, and extended family, I know love as it should be. Special thanks to Erin, Eileen, Jenny, Emma and William for their positive input and endless technical assistance. They are the new and improved models. Thank you to Liz and Richard for their keen eyes for detail. I love all of you.

My eternal thanks to my dear friends of the SC Writer's Association Surfside Chapter for their endless pool of knowledge and shared talents. Special thanks to Tibby, the Queen of Blubs, who has inspired me from day one. Kathleen is my wise one. Thank you for all the hundreds of questions you answered so kindly. Also, thanks to Bob who started me on the right path and Becky who answers my questions before I know the question. You make me smile.

I am forever indebted to and owe my sincere and heartfelt thanks to S C Retina Institute, Dr. Nick Marchase, Dr. Max Rumbaugh, nurse Lauren Gore, Kaylee Graves and staff for all the many miracles and kindness they have bestowed on me during this long hard-fought journey to save my vision. My gratitude is never ending.

Recipes

Norwegian Meatballs

(Kjøttkaker)

Ingredients
UNITS: **US**
Meatballs:

- 2 large eggs, lightly beaten
- 1 cup whole milk
- 1 cup dry breadcrumbs
- 1/2 cup finely chopped onion
- 2 teaspoons salt
- 2 teaspoons sugar
- 1/2 teaspoon each ground ginger, nutmeg, and allspice
- 1/4 teaspoon pepper
- 2 pounds extra-lean ground beef (95% lean)
- 1 pound ground pork

Gravy:

- 2 tablespoons finely chopped onion
- 3 tablespoons butter
- 5 tablespoons all-purpose flour
- 4 cups beef broth
- 1/2 cup heavy whipping cream
- Dash cayenne pepper
- Dash white pepper

Directions

1. In a large bowl, combine the eggs, milk, breadcrumbs, onion, and seasonings. Let stand until crumbs absorb milk. Add meat; stir until well blended. Shape into 1-in. meatballs.
2. Place meatballs on a greased rack in a shallow baking pan. Bake at 400° until browned, about 18 minutes or until a thermometer reads 160°; drain. Set aside.
3. For gravy, in a large skillet, sauté onion in butter until tender. Stir in flour and brown lightly. Slowly add broth; cook and stir until smooth and thickened. Blend in the cream, cayenne, and white pepper. Gently stir in meatballs; heat through but do not boil.

Norwegian Butter Cookies

(Serinakaker)

Ingredients
UNITS: **US**

- 3 1/2 cups all-purpose flour
- 1/2 teaspoon baking powder
- 1/2 teaspoon salt
- 1 1/2 cups butter, softened
- 1 cup sugar
- 2 tablespoons sugar
- 2 teaspoons vanilla
- 1 teaspoon almond extract
- 1 large egg, lightly beaten

Directions

1. Preheat oven to 350 degrees F.
2. Line a baking/cookie sheet with parchment paper.
3. In a medium bowl sift together flour with baking powder and salt.
4. In another bowl beat butter with 1 cup plus 2 tablespoons sugar, vanilla and almond extract until fluffy (about 3 minutes).
5. Add in egg and beat until combined.
6. Add in the flour mixture and beat on low speed until combined.
7. Form the dough into 1-1/2-inch balls.

8. Place the balls about 3-inches apart on the cookie sheet.
9. Using back of a fork flatten to about 1/2 to 1/2-inch thick making crisscross patterns.
10. Bake for about 10 minutes or until the edges are golden brown.
11. Transfer to wire racks to cool completely.
12. When the cookies are cooled coat lightly in confectioners' sugar, if desired.

Norwegian Christmas Bread

(Julelake)

Ingredients
UNITS: **US**
Bread:

- 1 cup butter (2 sticks)
- 2 cups scalded milk
- 1/4 teaspoon cardamom seeds, crushed
- 2 packets active dry yeast (4 1/2 teaspoons)
- 2/3 cup sugar divided
- 2 eggs, beaten
- 2 tablespoons grated orange zest
- 2 teaspoons salt
- 1 teaspoon cinnamon

- 6 cups all-purpose flour
- 2 to 3 cups dried or candied fruit (raisins, candied fruit, chopped maraschino cherries)
- 1 beaten egg for brushing

Icing:

- 2 cups confectioners' sugar
- 1/4 cup whole milk
- 2 tablespoons butter, melted
- 1/2 teaspoon almond extract
- Topping:
- Sliced almonds

Directions

1. To make the bread, in a small saucepan, melt the butter. Add the milk and scald. Remove from the heat and add the cardamom, letting the spice steep while the milk lowers in temperature to 110 degrees F.
2. In a mixing bowl, combine the yeast with 1/2 teaspoon of the sugar and pour a little of the lukewarm milk over them. Let proof until it bubbles, 5 to 10 minutes.
3. Stir in the remaining milk, along with the eggs, remaining sugar, the orange zest, salt, and cinnamon. Add 5 cups of flour and gently mix, adding additional small amounts until the dough begins to pull away from the sides of the bowl. (You may not need to use the full 6 cups of flour.)
4. Transfer to a lightly floured surface and knead for about 10 minutes. Fold in the dried fruit and transfer to a lightly

greased bowl. Cover with a clean tea towel and let rise until doubled, about 1 hour.

5. Punch down the dough and separate it into two equal portions. You can either place them in two greased 9-inch round cake pans or form them into two braided loaves. Cover with clean tea towels and let rise again until doubled, about 1 hour.

6. Preheat the oven to 375 degrees F.

7. Brush the loaves with the beaten egg and bake for 30 minutes, or until golden. Cool on a wire rack.

8. When cooled, to make the icing, sift the confectioners' sugar into a medium bowl, then add the milk, melted butter, and almond extract and whisk until smooth. Drizzle over the loaves, then scatter the sliced almonds on top. Let set before slicing.

Notes

Storage tip: Store extras wrapped in plastic at room temperature. When the bread starts to dry out, do yourself a favor and toast it, then smear it with butter, letting the butter melt into the cracks. Add *geitost*, too, if you have it. This is one of my favorite treats.